UNARMED AND DANGEROUS

Johns Hopkins: Poetry and Fiction

John T. Irwin
GENERAL EDITOR

Unarmed and Dangerous

NEW AND SELECTED POEMS

Wyatt Prunty

THE JOHNS HOPKINS

UNIVERSITY PRESS

Baltimore and London

This book has been brought to publication with the generous assistance of the Albert Dowling Trust.

The Johns Hopkins University Press
2715 North Charles Street
Baltimore, Maryland 21218-4363
www.press.jhu.edu

Library of Congress Cataloging-in-Publication
Data will be found at the end of this book.
A catalog record for this book is available from
the British Library.

ISBN 0-8018-6290-6

For Danny, Greg, Leah, and Phil

CONTENTS

WHAT WOMEN KNOW, WHAT MEN BELIEVE

New Poems

| The Downtown Bus

Out through the neighborhood with nothing more
Than home in mind, as the circling dog
Scuffs leaves along the curb, turns, sniffs, salutes,
Then races back then races off again,
Past Mrs. West who will not take the bus
But watches from her side yard where she waves
The passengers "good-bye" at seven-ten
And then "hello, hello" at five-fifteen,
When they unfold, walk forward, and step down,
Wait for the bus to clear, then eddy off
In twos and threes, take corners out of sight
As Mr. Probasco, who also waves,
Stands in his garden tying up the vine
That should have quit him weeks before, he says,
But keeps producing at its August best,

And the plain-faced houses lining the sidewalks
In shingled, bricked, and clapboard evidence,
And the half-bare oaks, colorful and gaunt,
As the street runs on, tunneling its limbs,
Or opening mid-block before the house
Where Wiggins sits, earmuffed in headphones,
Hunched with tuning his shortwave radio,
While next door Hooper's son honks through his sax
So the whole scale solos down into one
Long-complaining half-flat failing middle C
Which Wiggins hears through every frequency . . .
World News a monotone, Hooper's middle C,
Probasco standing halfway down his vine,
And Mrs. West, who knows its cancer, waving
The split infinitive of coming home.

Crosstown, home edges, creeps, and idles in
The evening traffic's legislative stop;
Indoors, it haunts from room to room as though
It were the echo, smell, uneven floor
Of parents primed and dressed for dinner out;
Side yard, it is the small self in the hedge
Half hidden like a lookout or a stray
Arrested in the quiet watchfulness
By which all cars slow to the one that stops,
Opens and admits into the sealed
Particular of simply going on;
     And now the downtown bus again, turning,
Slowing, braking to a door-wide rocking halt
With no one stepping off, only the driver,
Half cigarette and gravely bored,

Who checks his mirrors, elbows-in the door,
Then gazing absently, leans forward and shifts
Into the diesel's blue-smoke rag and wheeze
Throating its pleuritic, emphysemic sax
In hoarse successive half notes down the street—
So Hooper's middle C blends in, dissolves,
Then surfaces again, the bus rounding
A corner where its brake lights wink from sight,
As Mrs. West now drops her wave, turns back,
Probasco watching, whistling "Hi ho,"
She charting careful headway toward her porch
Till both hands pumping one-twos up the steps
She leans into the front door and it gives
As though the entire balance of the house
Angled where she fumbles for the light.

Inside's a speculation down one hall
Into another, then three connecting rooms

As one, two, three—three lights go on,
While up the street a gradual of yards
Filters the long, arterially fine light
Through back-stitched, overlapping twig and branch
Stripped to a half-leaf, clinging, patchwork spread
By which the many little depths of field,
The planes and verticals of home recede
Into the mild coagulum of now
Where sun and afternoon are going down
Into the brief remissions of four names—
Probasco, Hooper, Wiggins, Mrs. West,
Till even Hooper's son gives up his sax
In time for what already's happened next:

There was the downtown bus again, unscheduled,
Barging and bulking box-high down the street,
Ragged and loud, start-chug-stall-stop, start-stop,
Until the driver braked, climbed down, walked round,
And holding up the hood, "Flat dead," he said,
Next turned, eased five steps off, lit up; looked back:
But then Probasco there, toolbox in hand,
And the dog tugging, barking, and wagging,
And Wiggins, Hooper, Hooper's son under-
neath, and their eight legs sprawling randomly,
Four flashlights winking up through wires and hoses,
Each elbowing tools, all handing them round,
All talking in the tribal memory
Of how things work when they no longer work.

And then some loose wire tightened, the driver
Tried the door. Locked. Tried again; then looked instead,
Then waved the others over, who from the curb
Saw posture perfect, large-hatted and gloved
At ease behind the wheel and eyes ahead

Like Hepburn at the apex of her art,
Mrs. West, key in hand—who starting up,
Cocked her head, listened, touched the brake, sat tall,
Shoved into gear, then staring eagles through
The bug-pocked windshield's upright tinted glass
Accelerated hard, braked, cornered hard,
Wound the diesel tight again, circled back,
Slowing, waving, grinding gears, hitting the horn,
Block-round and waving and the horn going,
Dog barking, we five watching. Drove that way.
Drove all the late fall light from sight that way.

| Yes

> You know, when I'm sixteen I'm
> going to ride a motorcycle,
> swim in the deep end, and have
> jiggly breasts.   —Carolyn Ramseur, age 3

Always to see the world made whole,
Though that is just the thing it will not be,
The parent who looks back, suddenly old,
Or pet that walks the dark edge of the drive
Just out of sight and refusing when called;

And always to see the world made new,
A diver balancing, arms out, eyes fixed
Over the cold pool's undivided blue,
As sky-wide-high he now is rising down,
Feet up, head tucked, hands arrowheading into

The stilled then brightly-shattered surface
By which he either enters or disappears.
It is always either one or the other choice—
Heroes who go or just go away,
Through the sea, the jungle, some zeroed commonplace

We dream for them, with making the world whole.
As yes the tall-grass hatch of killdeer live
Because their parents play the vaudeville role
Of flutter, run, look back, limp, drag, and wait:
Parents and pets and years . . . all of it rolled

Into a longing neither sad
Nor quite wise to the loan's eventual terms;
As yes the chemo works, killing cells mad
And sane alike, as yes memory lives,
Collected, shelved, and waiting to unfold

When cross-town there's a siren going somewhere:
Hear all that urgent anonymity
Building and passing at once . . . to a fire,
A wreck, a false alarm or practical joke,
Or heart attack suddenly extravagant for air.

Hear each of these, both real and premature,
For Carolyn Ramseur, who, all of three,
Names the world and its manifold future,
Wanting to be what she sees as its glory—
The bike, the boobs, the deep-end's forfeiture—

Because there's something more that goes unsaid,
The dim flare of a candle guttering a wall
Whose liver-spotted water stains have bled
Years past a rafter's narrow crack of light.
Say yes to the candle stain's watery light.

I   The Old Cadets

Years later what they talked about was
The two who augured-in while taking off
And then the third who corkscrewed his landing
So in one day three planes stood nose down, tails up
Out at the corner of the field where fence
And fescue ruled and ran on boundary-long
Around the terse revisionary *nays*
No student liked to say—just thought all day—
Each factoring the edgy facts of what
Stalled in, malfunctioned, or *detached* could mean,
The last the best, *detached* sounding as though
Some prime umbilicus untied itself
So now no more the Chief's aggrieving roll
Or loud instructor's pimp for "gear adrift,"
Just three plowed planes with air-frames teetering
Like oversized, misjudged, abandoned toys.

Cadet Klietz joked about the Graveyard School
He'd read in school, who got it wrong, he said,
"Much better thinking fireworks on the Fourth . . ."
Which was the way the fourth one turned his earth,
Fire, smoke, the high-pitched diving whine; and Klietz,
Who now would always *almost* graduate,
A black flat jumble out in some farmer's field.
"A hard luck month," Commander Louis said,
As still the three planes augured in endured,
Patiently off balance at the runway's end,
Bright fabric ripped and rounded wafer-ribs
Bleaching white around three open cockpits
Yawning the boredom of those who went first.

And still the different distances ahead,
The skidding turn to final, power back,

9

Then cross wind and the cross-controlled descent,
Till lined up, nose high, wing dipped, rudder kicked,
It was float-wait, wait-float, touch, bounce, and roll out;
Or else it went the other way around:
Power and lift, and everything beneath,
Railroad, highway, and river meandering
Ahead, each but a brief installment of
The way you had to go—vector to course,
Minute to mile, the ticked infinity
By which you calculated drift and crabbed
Beyond mistakes like Klietz, totemed in the weeds.

Till those returning knew the ordinal
And ordinary route that got them out
And back and down to kick the tires again
(Not bad to kick the tires, light up, inhale),
Each having crossed that never-point that starts
The map's skewed plot and runway's drop from sight,
As gathering speed you hold on, climbing
From goggled embryo to wren's-egg-blue
To where you either learn or else you prove
An old man's fear of height and hope for altitude.

I Annals of Jack

Because Jack was small the world had to be large—
The Giant, the beanstalk, the lady in white
Charging Jack both to steal and restore,
Even Jack's appetite and the butcher's greed,
Or the prospect of the five bright beans which
Like Jack's father's death had to be buried
Before they could unfold their other world.

But the Giant really was big, you will say,
Big and hungry and living on the blood
Of Fee, Fi, Fo, and Fum, who passed through before
Our story and before the Giant's huge swallow
Tightened for some plug of an Englishman
Like Jack willing to crouch down in a stove
Or large pot where any second might mean the fire.

Plus there's something smart to say about the cow,
The way she goes from giving milk to being meat;
That, and the way the Giant's appetite dwarfs need,
As, false friend that he's been to Jack's dead dad,
He's left hungry and apprehensive.
Meanwhile, clever and cleaving, there's Jack to watch—
Stealing the hen, the eggs, and harp for mother.

And the Giant later? Imagine him not dead
But left behind, wandering the little-ease
Of ordinary rooms that open on
Halls tunneling revisionary doors,
Locked windows and the small prospects of fenced yards,
As Jack is now home, trickster, riddler,
But mildly deferential as the will's first

Parable for more than want, leaving the Giant
To mope through a hurt myopic blur of self
While Jack grows up good, meets Jill or Jackie,

11

And never again tools around for favor,
Which means never again climbs from this world
But shoulders alone the valleyed wilderness
Of a dead father and his own dying itch.

How to describe what you mostly don't live—
Gliders and swings spaced geometrically
Across the close-cut, agreed-upon lawn
Where sunset recaptures you beautifully
Simply for seeing the extended light
Of one stalled ending? It's endings after all.
Ask anyone waiting. Or looking ahead.
Ask Jack, Giant descending, when he chops down the stalk.

But sometimes at dinner Jack forgets to ask,
And out of his sleeve the hairy forearm
Stretches twice its natural length, hand hovering
Paw-like just above the food. Then catching
Himself, Jack pulls it back, twines his fingers, waits,
Seated at what is either the head or the end
Of a tired reproduction Chippendale.

And sometimes too, in bed before he sleeps,
Jack sees the five bright beans and generous stalk
Unfolding so the minor miracle
Repeats itself, as waking-child again
He reaches through the high-leafed promise
Of five small deaths, either discarded
Or planted, each for a dry cow
That was a hen, a harp, hope out of hunger,
And all the dim gold of a lifetime.

| A Child's Christmas in Georgia, 1953

Marching through Georgia to bed, he stopped, listened,
And heard, "While shepherds washed their socks by night."
Later, he sang the same skewed line off key,
And his parents howled; until getting it wrong,
He decided, beat getting it right.

But Christmas Eve they read about killing
The first-born, fleeing the land, and returning
By another country, till he couldn't sleep
And had to check so slipped from bed to stare
The darkened height by which the wise men steered.

Downstairs there were his mother's stacks of albums
And, mantle-high, her unblinking gallery
Of gold-framed graybeards gazing, and matriarchs
In black, scowling the generations back
Into place; and then there were the others,

His infant older brother who never
Came home, two cousins lost in war, an uncle
Who captained his ship over the flat world's edge,
And one fleece-lined pilot lost years now inside
The stilled weather of a relative's box camera.

And then there were the lines he'd heard in church,
"Pray that your flight may not be in winter,"
So that was how the pilot disappeared?
And "Woe to the pregnant and nursing," so
That explained his brother, or their mother?

There was one thing he knew by heart by now:
Rubella cooked, cleaned, and scolded her way
Through the house tuning the news and talking back,
Though she didn't vote, and said her baby
Died because he wouldn't come out in Georgia.

Still standing there and staring up, he pressed
His face till the cold glass fogged and hurt his nose,
Though there was only the street light yellowing
The side yard and his father's dormant garden
And the Talmadges' coiled drive and empty house.

So what were they singing about, the records
And radio? And why all these presents
When over drinks his parents grieved those missing?
What was given if you had to go away
And wound up framed like a silent question?

In the morning Rubella would light the stove;
The paper boy would whistle up Milledge,
Tossing the new day high over one hedge
Into another by the porch for parents
Who ignored their food and read to themselves.

So, still at the window, he studied the sky,
Figuring Pontius Pilate flew for Delta
And that the two parts to the Bible were
The Old and New Estimates, which like Christmas
You read out of the names of those missing.

Extravagant Love

Irritated and sometimes utterly through
With it all, they've wound up in the hushed stacks
Of Last-Will-and-Word, having turned the zoo
Of self so inside-out they've settled back
To elements as gritty as Birmingham
And totally lacking in what ginned
Up names like Larkin, Nemerov, and Cunningham—
Whom the keepers had no chance of keeping in
Till now, when one of them walking the aisles
Pulls down a book, leafs through the leaves, and reads
That the Old Fools made love in the flat style
And wormed their dogs in the operatic hush of the dead:

Takes getting used to, three foxed S-O-B's
Whose best lines run across the page like scars
Carved in the tree of us healing crookedly
Over the dead foliage of who we are.

I The Books

Behind what they said, he always thought that they
Didn't mean to warn him once but forever,
As leaving them opened on the couch or floor
He'd stop and rehearse all their unfolding truths
And see how there would never be enough
To write the hero's end. At night, picked up
And shelved by alphabet above his bed,
They rested, ready to open again
Mid-air and drifting out across the room,
While he, sent off to sleep, would always ask
For the Big Records, old seventy-eights
He knew by every scratch and warp-unfolding pause—

He who wanted all the stories read at once,
Fearing the cracked world whispered through a wall
Made of its many words that spoke themselves
Just like the lost who would not listen to
The cautionary tale all stories told—
He who thought at last the books would tell him
Why people couldn't stay, and how their maps
Unraveled into ink-dissolving roads,
While the sleepless boy and hall light stood watch,
And the sleepless books crowded their shelves all night,
Cover to corner to closed-disclosing end,
Silently saying, "By this, I mean that;
So when you walk here, you have traveled there."

| March

Seeing the March rain flood a field
So suddenly the water stands
Seeping from sight, while at the fence
The wind rags up a bare-limbed argument
On which a hawk rises, circles,
Then pumps from sight under clouds clotted
And driven so the bunched low sky
Stampedes in blundering shapes
So changeable they disprove shape—
And then the rain again, in which
The clouds come down but differently,
Driven and driving, blunted or edged,
As now how will it be when what
We call a shift in season
Blusters, or storms, or goes dead still
With us left standing underneath
To wonder or ignore the change
From overhead to underfoot,
Going on regardless where we've gone,
Who we were, what we ever said or did?

1 Oh General, Oh Spy, Oh Bureaucrat!

You son of a bitch. What are you trying to do? Destroy
Eisenhower? —"Beedle" Smith

Trained in tactics, war games, cold war, cold feet,
Baroque what-ifs against a failing East,
And History a venality of names
By which Max Weber, Calvin, or King James
Would profit faith into bureaucracy,
Busyness, business, hope's tucked property—
He made long lists, committeed the abyss
Of time unbuttoning a hidden proof
Discovered like an army in which gain
Is truculence, promotion, sometimes truth,
But elsewhere only soldiers on those trains
That ended derailed, deserted, and sometimes missed.

| The Poem

Gnarled avenues the years have mapped
In mazed geometries, iterant gaps,
While August heat has baked the lake beds dry,
Jigsaw and moonscape cratered in the eye—

The little thief survives by going on
Through emptied states whose borders run
A river valley's scouring descent
Beneath the sundial-pine's flecked monument,

To where light masses in the shrug of one
Low limb, and water speaks the rounded stone
That says, the river's syllabled by force
And all the down it drives repeats its source,

Which once the riffle, rift, or eddy stills
Restores the clear pool's cold suspended will.

1 Since the Noon Mail Stopped

This

Gust blustering, and the March rain
Loosening its chill percussive tap
A thousand pockmarks up the drive,
Crossing where the silt dust gives to grass
So only sound—till that gone too,
As a single crow glides south-southeast,
Chasing some few bruised clouds on a wind
Plundering the low sky's crazy shapes,

And then the valance-down blue virga
Dropping from its shelf of clouds
And disappearing midway up,
As though by falling all might rise
And rising fall again above
The knuckling roots' blind budge
And mineral buckling out into
That web where mole and shrew will wait,

As now a new gust rolling through,
And the long rain reaching fully down,
Scattering and cold, mining the roof,
Runneling the yard, tenpenny hard
Its hammering hiss, saying, this, this, this.

The Pyromaniac

A one-story is disheartening,
Brief unelaborated light building
Under eaves, traveling sideways, gulping air,
And the slow smoke bellying after.
Three stories, four, five, or more work best
For my hushed start, in which the rest
Becomes a climbing fall toward light,
The blue flame's leap to furnace white
And stoked accumulation where
Hunger lives on hunger, hollowing air
As the dicing flames still time,
As empty coats, arms bent in pantomime,
Go up, as my two shoes tip up, their toes
Curled the way I make whole buildings go—
Out of the rich gas and fire's brief bright
Dancing its combustible light
On top of light, as if it drew
The nail-board-mortar of all lives into
One hot cumulus billowing from below.

That's why I strike the match, that I may know
No god's revenge for fire, but my own,
My own curled side bent to a stone
As obdurate and blank as hate,
Although not for some dark bird's appetite,
I have my own of that, instead the flame,
Consuming everything the same
Till nothing offers more of hope
Than gas-soaked rags, the building smoke
That hides its fire so rising whole
Bright tongues curl into coals
As air shafts roar and windows amplify
How high my hungry bright will bite the sky.

| The Sneeze

The first day sleet, the second ice,
And nothing moved, till going for the mail
I stepped, slipped, sailed, heels high, higher,
So blue sky over toes, wide spastic arms,
And shoulder blades blunt anviling the ice—

Where when I hit the spine-long back of me
Some tearing cloth gave out along its seam
As though a child's hand crushed dry cereal.
And then the building cold beneath. Then nothing.

Next I was back and rolling to my side
So right arm down and set and legs balled tight
I elbowed up. Then wrist-to-hand, tucked feet,
Half stood, balanced, looked around, teetered, slipped;
And it was loose-hinged limp and rubber down.
Lay curled again. Till, knees-to-belly rising,
Feet beneath, I angled up, legs half bent,
Straightened, compassed one way, leaned the other,
Then shuffle-side-stepped, see-saw-armed-it home.

And now for three taut weeks there's been this change:
First eyes tight-sponged and lungs ballooning up
The room inflates, then I am round-eyed huge
As everything I see. And then the sneeze.
And the fine tight grinding mesh goes off again.
Somewhere a small foot scuffs leaves. Goes on.

| The Window Washer

The daily way for looking is inside.
But once a woman glared at him, stripped herself,
Then walked across the room, sat down, and cried;
He stalled midair, astounded on the shelf
Of that blue self,

Till paying out his rope and working down
He bumped to where he'd started off, loose ride
Back to the sidewalk, street, and vacant ground
Long his before he ever tried
Two intervening sides.

Then he was back, washing the mirrored blue
Of all he saw—within, the dollhouse walls
And offices, and people passing through
To sometimes stop and answer calls,
Then walk the halls.

Till now two lines spaghetti cross the top,
Sway back and forth, settle and descend,
Green paying out till red belays the stop,
And movement is a pendulum that ends
Where it begins:

Then he kicks off, swings back, pumps up momentum,
Fanning by so sometimes looking in
And sometimes out, thanks to the sky-blue sum
The glass has taught, reflecting him,
Silent and thin;

As some days all he thinks is frame to frame,
Cleaning until it seems there's no one there,
Nor glass between, but everything the same,
Till he has washed and dried the air
Of nowhere.

A Baseball Team of Unknown Navy Pilots, Pacific Theater, 1944

Assigned a week's good bunt, run, throw,
Makeshift uniforms, long practices,
Then games, playoffs, and a round of photos
Stark as this one slipping from its frame,
Where hats, gloves, bats in hand these stood
Lined up and focused, smiling and unnamed—

Till the shutter clicked and each went back,
Retracing zagged geometries
Of the navigator's elbowed tack
And smudged replotted overrule
Pulled from a fix when miles off track
They crabbed the wind and calculated fuel;

And then the wide sleek secret fleet below
Blacked out until the climbing tracers
Sent their bright concussive flak
And going on was all. Time wound,
And some planes banking, others not;
And the one, tail-riddled, easing down,

Crew tossing weight for altitude
Till smoke and someone spelling out a fix.
Then static graveling the words.
And still these faces, whose names we never got,
As all we know is they returned to bases,
Went up when told, came home or not.

I Sequence

Sang off-key so mouthed the words,
Looked judicious when he couldn't hear,
What he forgot claimed he didn't need,
Avoided mirrors and biographies,
Read the sports and rarely finished,
Never listened but liked to talk.

Pushed when the door said Pull,
Eavesdropped on telephones,
Blew his nose on linen napkins;
Had a dog he couldn't call,
Built a house he didn't finish,
Had a job he never named,
Thought his father's life was sad.

Chewed rubber bands, sucked spaghetti,
Parked in handicapped slots,
Jammed the meter with slugs,
Backed without looking,
Braked on ice, and sometimes late at night
Drove on the wrong side laughing,
Laughing on the wrong side all the way home.

I Zamboni's Law

Shave, water, scrub, and sweep the rink
Of all the etched meanderings
By which the skaters enter their
Broad cursives on the ice;
Play the music slow or play it fast,
Then turn the lights until you see
That only by Zamboni things agree.

Knife round and round the ice those O's
Whose widened emptiness controls
The way a skater's clockwise run
Gives out before the law.
Let tickets flood across the gates,
As now the skaters race to learn
All is erased when it's Zamboni's turn;

As now the slow-curved couples pass,
Nodding and talking, wobbling on,
And the overtaking singles
Pumping and weaving ahead,
Till coming round again they lean
Angled for that opening whose good
Is that Zamboni's law stands understood—

When the foghorn warning sounds its bass
Expelling each beyond the ice
So all stall mute outside the wall,
Watching how the blue, bulked, boxy grind
Restores a hardened glaze
As cold and clear as any thought we keep
To save Zamboni's law from how Zamboni sweeps.

| Eyeing the World

Furtive the hedgerow cat
Crouched watchfully wise
At the field's far edge, as fat
As suspicious behind bright eyes

That study the rows
For rabbit and shrew, mouse or mole
Shrinking in shadows,
Wing-scything shadows that circle,

Descend, till the cat curls small
To see what follows—
The hawk's wings sprawled
As it tears, swallows,

A dark-phase bird
Wide over a shrew,
And eyeing the world
For anything new

In the casual field;
Till the hawk now done
Folds in its wings, hops,
Flaps up, and climbs the sun;

Leaving the bones
And the cat's crouched wonder
At death's high ocean
Of light and hunger.

| Coach

All trucks were from Hell and deserved my bite,
All children sheep and not to leave the yard.
Before I came, the house was unsafe;
The man whistled and no one heard,
And the huge trucks lumbered.

When the boy walked out, ball in hand,
I coached. He called me that. "Coach,"
He'd say, and I'd bark back, "Now! Now!"
Till the game was "Here Coach, Fetch Coach,"
And I was off and straightway back, unless,
Of course, one of the trucks from Hell passed by.

Thrown objects were my specialty,
The lazy sticks, their high trajectories,
That, and the knack I had for words—
Here, fetch, hunt, stay, sit, lie-down . . .
And names, for the boy, his sister.
I lived those names twelve years, a diplomat
Who read the world four different ways,
Nose, ear, eye, and sometimes what was said.

When my coat thinned, legs stiffened, and I
Turned deaf, I was practical; I didn't run,
Limped wisely over, once the stick had plopped.
Then the children left, as sticks were lost,
As the man's whistle rose past hearing,
As all sounds stopped, and I was nose and eye,
Watching the trucks from Hell roll by,
Each silent and deserving of my bite,
Which the last one got, till I never let go.

The Sorrows of Lester Buster

First there were the trips, the cars, then girls;
And following that an ennui like sap
Sticking to every sentence he unfurled,
His welling forth become her dripping tap

Till balding faster than he could gray,
He said he wanted his autonomy;
And so she let him go his way, away,
Not even asking alimony.

Then he returned, having grown, he said . . . and changed.
But she had got the habit of the feel
Of being free, though she offered to arrange
A separate room, trying to smile.

But he was ardently back, he said;
So she subscribed to the daily as his wife,
Frying his eggs, bacon, steaks, and skillet breads,
Freezing the desserts he liked about his life,

As along it went, his middle age,
Muddling on for a year or two,
Until she said, "All the world's a stage
You're passing through."

And he was, through that is, dead in the act,
In a motel on the edge of town—
No girl left, fictitious names for facts,
Only his old stiff self to pin him down.

Outside, the flashing lights went round and round
To the sirens, radios, phones, and the sound
Of cameras and the gurney unfolding,
As someone took her arm and she was holding

A plastic bag with watch, wallet, ring.
"Can you identify these things?"
He wanted to know, "Were they, the, his, effects?"
She stood, as though waiting for the next

Installment. Later, some neighbors standing by
Saw her son pull up, hop out, get the door,
Then heard her say while waving them good-bye,
"I think a little sooner's always better."

I   Recovery

That elbow with its pinpoint bruise
Just where the ligament tore loose,
Or herniated disk, pancaked sideways
And threatening to stay that way
So you're a sorry manikin for clothes
Who bending stiffly down to hoist his bags
Stays put, until the comedy allows
That someone bend to bend you up again;

Then bone spur knuckled into nerve
So arm shoots pain and fingers numb,
Or spasm through the neck so head clocks down,
Stilled in rigid compensation;
Gimp knee, arthritic toe, a touch of gout,
And off you go, but differently,
Until, gout gone, you tiptoe after.

That is the mystery by which the late pain
Walks a later floor, answers each new step,
And punctuates tomorrow's tense,
As with a rib's caught breath, carved shape;
Or emphysema quantifying stairs,
So every step's a calisthenic now
Collected on its miniature abyss—

Where the crooked elbow can't unbend
And arm goes only so much high,
Where the football knee that never kneels
Unhinges and rehinges equally,
Where winter-long the twisted spine perfects its coat,
As all my life I thought shape shrouded form
And form was full, but where we wince
As though called back we hollow how we go.

I Seasons

At tennis, a missed shot meant he had MS.
Later, over drinks it was the Big Bands,
Night trains, DC 3's, Packards—an express
Of images held headlong out of hand
In what he called his photogenic memory.
No one corrected. Dinner went well.
But seeing him to his car, he turned to me,
Arms shrugging outward, "What the hell,
Someone stole the Packard. Go call the cops."
Settled in his Buick, window powered down,
He leaned out confidentially, "Dumb slobs,
Putting all this plastic in a Packard."
                                        Then he was gone,
And I stood waving, after what? Self-referee
Of a widower and skeptic who when asked
Said, "You believe in clear because it's cloudy."
Ten years alone and nothing of hers packed.
"All charities are scams," he said. "Clear
Us both out all at once. We go together—"
As the Packard or Buick steered a few more years,
Gathering dents inexplicable as weather
And he renamed his tennis, "Rigorous Mortis."

A few late trips; mostly cruises.
But once, a full-blown bash with all the downstairs
Opened wide, bars on porches, in the yard,
And the Big Bands going long past goodnights
And the last few cars turning hard
To clear the drive and accelerate from sight.

House empty, cigar stoked, he went about
Puffing, fly down, shirt tail out, blowing smoke
At windowpanes, watching the cloudbanks go,
Each fanning past its glass. Until the last,

In which the smoke resolved him mirrored in
The single pane that told the backward joke
Which, nothing like its small spent storm of dark,
Cleared after him the hall and only stairs
Climbing the whole house rigidly from sight.

The Razed House

Take the steep stairs up to where the rafters meet
And fan back down into the eaves
Like abstract tepees hung beneath
The ridgepole height and attic reach
Of a roof that hides what holds it up,
A maze of canted tensions,
King post, tie beam, purlin, strut.
Walk on the loosely slatted floor, testing
The syncopated clack and sway of beam one way
And unnailed plank the other, while beneath,
Calamitously poised, nested mice
Listen in the runneling snugs of the floor's dark length.

Or go three floors back down the way you climbed
To the burrowed basement darkening from sight,
Where the landing stalls and sunless slab
Opens on abandonment—corners cobwebbed
And flecked with wings on fretwork lines;
And beneath, here and there gnawed exits where
Rats stretch and wedge coaxial spines—
Sometimes a hole as circular and true
As if by template, yet empty as retreat;
And once, high in the wall, the delicate crest
Of a small skull, and ribs woven
In the briared lattice of an abandoned nest.

Between the scaled extremes of high and low
There's carpet and the polished wood
Of what you know, walking the average day
That voids its shadows—as the sprinkler goes,
A boy passes, arcs his paper, hears it plop,
And a dog wakes, collects his tongue, stands,
Stretches, watching a school bus yellow its stop,
Barged halt and flapping folding door

Till no one's there; and the wheels turn
And gears thrum, beyond the blue exhaust blown
Sideways and lingering like the spent gesture
Of a struck match, doused fire, someone alone.

Rise in the dark, pull on the clothes you wore
The day before, then pad out through the house,
Not seeing the table, chair, breakfront, sideboard
But sensing certain densities along a floor
You know by heart—till there's the rocker, stilled
And tilting back before the window where
The first light fills your sill;
And the yard resolves,
Its terraced beds edging into color
As though the green world woke restored again. As though.
And a car passes, lights pushing two white bowls
Of the concrete over which it rolls.

No architect comes after where you walk;
Only the rooms, whose walls are echoes of
A self-repeating voice that names its way
As if it made the woodwork talk.
But a nail, backed out from driven in,
Catches your sleeve as often as you pass;
Hammer it home, the wood will twist it out again.

And the windows, whose glass ripples and runs
Like water over glass, they stand
Immovably blank, neither cluttered nor clear,
Painted into their frames so the lattice holds
Two worlds at once—rooms you walk, and the yard's high air
In which the afternoon stretches overhead,
Filling the elbowed branching trees

As now you hear a few dry leaves
Blown edgewise scraping up the wall
Into the vaulted high of one hard gust
So circling they widen, drop.
                            You know
The end is the end when the numbers change,
Phone and address; and never other name
But as you'd spell abandonment;
Till the walls come down and fill the basement up,
And the workers leave, some looking back, some not,
And you're a quiet sentence, a harbored thought.

| Since the Noon Mail Stopped

Once upon a time, when the clocks were slow
And windows tall with all I didn't know,
One thing confirmed the ordinary day
And taught me how the grown-up world would stay.

The mail fell from its secret in the door,
Silent and leaflike, loose along the floor,
And always someone gathered it from there,
Explaining all that *big* that came from *where*

As though each correspondence mapped a route
Beyond the origins of hidden doubt.
And of the ones who answered that address
Nothing's changed their opening from this:

Now that there's no delivery for here,
And those who've walked ahead have turned and stare,
I write the names for whom the letters drop
Unchanging where the noon mail stops.

Reading before We Read, Horoscope and Weather

My father laughing over the morning paper
Where the written world fell open on the funnies,
Manic sports, stalled politics . . . and where
The Horoscope said, "now," the Forecast, "sunny,"

He couldn't laugh enough, so skipped a page,
Then another, till the back door shut,
An engine turned, and I woke up his age
In the mirror of a gray no scissors cut.

He backed out of his pulling in at night
As light elbowed past an opened door, failing
Down six empty steps. Now a wall-switch bites
Blue sparks before the neon's billowing

Over another kitchen's white-on-white
Enameling; and now the sun is up
And climbing through the windows to a height
I follow out and off beyond the steep

Fence and trees to where the sky cuts flat
And blank as the paper spread in front of him,
My father then, waiting till I'd padded in, pulled out
My chair, inched up, and yawned that he begin.

Nothing is as funny now as then.
Still, when they rumple in, they bring his eyes
And mine, squinting and wet with laughing
Over the cracked, cracked up, sidewise, unwise

Stories that I read to them, telling how
We bend, break, wires shorting, knotting and strange;
Never as the Horoscope's predicted "now,"
But as the weather comes, fresh and ignorant of change.

| Thaumatrope

And sometimes there's this parlor trick;
One side spider, other side the web,
Then thread pulled so the small card spins
And two sides turn to one.
                          How obvious
And unrehearsed this seems, as darkened glass
Both mirrors and obscures, as pilots think
Blue water must mean bluer sky,
Till climbing up that unknown down
They enter their full-fathomed fall;

As though the world remained the world because
One seeing found the many ways agree—
The first six colors hidden in pastel,
Primary letters rounding into script,
As we have read the double agent's name
That buried in obits or in an ad
Was neither signature nor side.

The Crows

There were the cautionary crows
Complaining tree to tree. He moved below,
Watching them lumber into the air,
Lifting and lighting, alone, in pairs,
Till lazing off in ragged echelons
They climbed, thinned from sight, and were gone—
As though the black of them were soluble,
Their outward empty wings as probable
As where he crouched, picking through the used,
Forgotten, broken, and refused
Collection of the entire town's slagged junk,
Last week already dozed and steeply sunk
But for a bookcase, couch, and chair
Piled near a bedstead heading up the air.

Across the way his leaning truck
Waited for the sum of what he'd lug,
Its cluttered bed already stacked with tires,
Shutters, axles, spools of wire.
But then he saw the high returning crows,
Lined up, stretched, lumbering and slow,
Till rounding down they tightened, dropped,
Opened, settled, heads cocked.
And then the one hopped up, the others flapped,
As they seesaw-walked it toward a strip
Of something only they could see.
Circling, they picked it patiently.

And the man forgetting what he held
And turning from the high truck's tilting load
Stepped sideways for a closer look—
One foot, another; till the crows spooked.
And all their metal voices rose,
Wings banking sideways out and low

As though they'd angle back for more,
Of what they found so rich before.

And he stood where he sized the ground.
Nothing. Bits of paper floating down,
Light scratch-marks crisscrossed through the dust,
That momently blew nowhere in a gust;
Till bending close, pushing aside some trash,
He saw the bones, dark hair, and ash.
Then he was in his truck and working gears
Ahead into the bug-flecked windshield's smear,
As farther back still stood the trees,
Motionless and black, shadowing degrees
By which the day went on beneath a sun
That only meant the sun, now that the crows were done.

| Late Fall, Late Light

As if an army rose out of one grave
Though not out of one wish but millions,
So looking back the landscape widened till
Each field became its own rich opening
Beside a round-top country road
Running its long down-backwards slowly home,

And the loose-leaf look of it, all afternoon,
Firing October's brilliant camouflage,
Holding the late light brighter where
It breaks between the rounding reds and yellows,
A thousand brief illuminated stops
So leaf to limb to trunk to undergrowth
The light collects in variegated shades
That deepen where they spread,
While overhead the round-eyed sky
That never blinks but eyes us blindly on
Goes on as bluely blank as ever,
Till the low sun levels through the trees,
Its thousand changes burning into one.

| The Tent

Too serious above his opened book,
Our father told us not to whisper a word,
So everything we said we had to shout,
As running for the phone and answering
With "She's out to the barn to milk the cows,"
Or "He's off with his mother sewing clothes,"
We'd hoof it up and down the hardwood hall,
Rip arguments, then pound the bedroom walls,
Stomp up and down the stairs, slam doors, bang drawers,

Until he came home with the tent from Sears
And, busying past every question why,
Scanned the instructions, arched them for the trash,
Then propped two poles and started pounding stakes.

So next the soft green boxy sag was up—
And the brand-new Coleman and folding chair;
Then for the two months left that summer
Our father finished dinner, walked outside,
Nursed the hissing Coleman up to bright,
And, opening the folding chair, took out his book.

At first our mother watched him from the door,
But then gave backwards to the living room
Where even we now entered quietly.
At dusk, neighbors driving home slowed and stared
At the tent's green square and small white door,
Our father leaning forward in the light
As the high astringent failing sky bled dark
And underneath the tent glared on.

Back in the house we hoofed about more slowly,
Spoke less, and steered around our arguments,

Agreed to leave the TV volume low,
Quit dawdling and stumped to bed on time.

And never knew just when the lamp went out,
As silent in our sleep the back screen swung
First one way then the other, as whoever
Walked back in decided he would stay.

The Foliage Tour

1

We climb, the changes changing rapidly—
Tired greens, then yellows, orange, red, then green again;
"Forevergreen," says the man beside me;
Gauze for a cap and propped into a cane,
Raising his hand, touching where no hair remains.

He asks, "And what about your family?"
"In front," I point. We count three bobbing heads,
As the bus shifts down. And now it's up and slowly
Between the always evergreen he said—
Before we counted heads.

"And yours?" I ask mechanically.
"Just one, and she's gone on for now."
He says that carefully, studying me,
Waiting to hear me ask what I would know,
"Where did she go?"

But when I ask he only smiles,
Looking up the aisle as though the future tense
Climbed a road up through the fall for miles,
And no way left to stop, or turn the distance
To anything but distance.

2

Then we were coasting down the way we came,
Out of the evergreens, back to the range
Of red, orange, yellow—all different and the same,
As he was telling me the thing most strange
Was that the doctors changed.

So he checked out and started out,
Touring on the hope, or the belief in hope,
That he was well, "up and about,"
He said, "well as before; cresting slopes
And never out of rope."

Rope raveling like reason on a guess
And never any word for loss
Except percentages—more, less,
Maybe a few months more, dice tossed
And the odds at any cost . . .

As we, ticketed, bussed, and bland,
Became the road and whining wheels beneath
The ticking trees whose fractions were the land
We rode to see, all colors one, leaves and a leaf,
Shadow and belief.

I Cold

Another front, sleet, snow, and the feeder
Leaning in a wind cranking from the north
And tanking coldly in all afternoon,
As I have carried seed and scattered seed,
Built piles of brush with more seed underneath,
While overhead and off to every side
The junkos, siskins, cardinals, thrashers wait
For my huffed pumping back indoors again:
Then the hushed world darting down, some gliding,
Others slipping sideways in to land, stand,
Go marching, cocked heads angling for food.

Later, a storm of blackbirds clots the sky—
Huge clogged formations banking left and right,
Then darting low, skimming the limbs and gone,
As two large crows have folded in and walk
A black ellipse of seeds across the snow;
Till even the crows are up, rowing darkly,
And something larger circling above,
Its tipped wings widening with rounding down.

I watch the hedge where all the locals hide,
Limbs stitched so's not a cardinal's hood in sight,
As now the hawk glides in, bends, seizes a limb.
Another thirty minutes means full dark.

But then the hawk is off and up the wind,
Rising and banking, circling higher, gone,
And all the locals piling it back in,
So many reds and grays darting through limbs,
And something new, a goldfinch here, there; hidden.

As the light bleeds out along an angled shaft
The kitchen window throws across the snow

Where wing by wing the count ticks off to one
Gray junko hunched inside the feeder's base
And working through what's left so he can last
A night well on its way down under zero.
He rustles, kicks; the feeder twists.
I watch to see which way he'll fly. He stays.

And then it was so dark his flying went
Hiddenly beyond my looking out,
As suddenly the wind was all I knew,
And the window's light, flooding back the snow;
And farther, the feeder swaying emptily,
As gray to darker gray to dark itself
Something had gone that I wished beyond reason.

| Stick Builder

Hammer, nail, and board I go, pounding
Without blueprints so stud, joist, and rafter meet
As though I built by ear; stout hammering
And saw that say I know board feet
By the shapes they take, each room expanding
Six ways from two hands, until complete.
As now the whole house stands complete, waiting
Those who moving in will sleep and eat
Inside the idea I have built for them,
Which is as close as I will ever live to them.
That's why, finishing, I sign and write, "Stick Built." So
Someday cleaning out their attic they will know
Whose hand was here before there was a here,
Who built by touch so like touch he was near.

| Four Winter Flies

Lost and stumbling across the window,
They want the light that looks like warmth until
I lift the sash and off they go,
Blown in a brief cold gust that stuns, its chill

Leaving them slow to recover. Then they return,
Dotting the glass, tracing what they cannot touch
Until they're vacuumed up and out to turn
Into the earth for which they've swarmed so much.

May each buzz back behind its thousand eyes
To pace the unforgiving pane where sight
Said "come" and it could not and died,
As all die, opposite the world's long light

Whose bare-limbed seepage and shallowing rise
Once proved the brief ellipsis of four late flies.

| Grown Men at Touch

Of the barn's shadow we declared our field.
The ball, six to a side, and two-hand-touch
Went anywhere the barn's broad shadow stretched:
It grew flat wide out of the eastern side
All afternoon. By four, our shadow-field
Had gone long past the longest pass;
By five, no one could run its length.
Across the eastern grass the barn squared black
And increased as the sun sank low, so slant
Was all the light we had, and the long field
Longer still.
                    Play only means because it ends.
But here the field ran on, out to the next field
And the next, as shadow shaded into dark
So fences disappeared, roads sank, trees blanked.
And there was no way now to stop the game
In which one play means miles out through a night
That turns a stare blind wide of sight
With searching out the grown-up trick
By which you don't see and you never quit.

I   The Funerals

You'd think we'd have them down by now,
Dark suits and all that driving back and forth
And walking in and walking out again
With hearing yet another's lost his lines
Somewhere inside the never-plot's last turn
Where "good show" equals "dumb show" equals "end."

Instead, there's but the low sun through the door,
And the sundial floor telling what comes next,
As tile-by-tile the light grows long beneath
Us solemn few who fill the rows and watch
Our shadows climb the wall's blunt vertical,
Where later on it does no harm that when
We size the stone on which the last word's etched
We mind the light and skip the epitaph.

I The Run of the House

| Haying

They are gathering hay. The truck rolls slowly.
The men walk on either side, lifting bales,
Talking without looking up. When one truck fills
Another takes its place, the loaded truck
Turning for the barn, where another crew waits
To get the bales up to the loft.
                              There is a boy
They've hired for one day; he gets half wages.
They've put him at the top where it's hot,
Where he drags the bales from the lazy belt.
He can't lift the bales, so he backs then tugs,
Backs then tugs, feeling the barn's tin roof bake down.

They've worked since 6 A.M. and now the sun
Enlarges through the trees, which line the field's
Far edge, where the other crew follows a truck.
The older men wear overalls; the young men
Are stripped to the waist. The boy still wears his shirt.
Twice he has tried tobacco, twice gotten sick,
But now he is tired and elated,
Seeing the field's last load turning towards the barn.

Then tugging a bale, he brushes the nest.
And there are yellow jackets everywhere.
And the stings are everywhere, under his shirt,
On his ears, down each arm, and he is running,
Tripping, stung, running again, stung, climbing
Through the stings and rolling along the loft,
Another sting, and the loft's floor opening

And he sees the battered truck, the men circled
And he is on the truck's bed looking up,
The men still circled, and gazing down.
They don't move him, they will not move him,

And he can't move himself.
                    Old Smythe bends near
And puts tobacco on the stings.
He breaks a cigarette, chews the tobacco,
Then puts it on a sting—here, there, another . . .
Then another cigarette.
                    He asks the boy
Can he move his legs. The boy says, no,
Yes, maybe . . . maybe in a minute.

The men talk on, as calmly as before—
Complain about the heat, swat flies, light up.
The doctor's on his way and it's all right
Because they meant to quit, needed to,
Else they would have started the next field
And never gotten home.
                    Lie there, boy,
And listen to their neutral voices—
Used for selecting seed, planting, calving,
Used when wringing necks or cutting calves to steers,
Used for harvest, slaughter, funerals, drought—
And August always turns to drought,
One baking gust that cures the grass
Like a breath inhaled and held
So long that light turns colors.

I   The Ferris Wheel

The rounding steeps and jostles were one thing;
And he held tight with so much circling.
The pancaked earth came magnifying up,
Then shrank, as climbing backward to the top
He looked ahead for something in the fields
To stabilize the wheel.

Sometimes it stopped. The chairs rocked back and forth,
As couples holding hands got off
And others climbed into the empty chairs;
Then they were turning, singles, pairs,
Rising, falling through everything they saw,
Whatever thing they saw.

Below—the crowd, a holiday of shirts,
Straw hats, balloons, and brightly colored skirts,
So beautiful, he thought, looking down now,
While the stubborn wheel ground on, as to allow
Some stark monotony within,
For those festooned along the rim.

The engine, axle, spokes, and gears were rigged
So at the top the chairs danced tipsy jigs,
A teetering both balanced and extreme,
"Oh no," the couples cried, laughing, "Stop!" they screamed
Over the rounding down they rode along,
Centrifugal and holding on.

And he held too, thinking maybe happiness
Was simply going on, kept up unless
The wheel slowed or stopped for good. Otherwise,
There were the voices, expectant of surprise;
Funny to hear, he thought, their cries, always late,
Each time the wheel would hesitate,

Since the genius of the wheel was accident,
The always-almost that hadn't,
A minor agony rehearsed as fun
While the lights came up and dark replaced the sun,
Seeming to complete their going round all day,
Paying to be turned that way.

Later, standing off, he felt the wheel's mild dread,
Going as though it lapped the miles ahead
And rolled them up into the cloudless black,
While those who rode accelerated back
And up into the night's steep zero-G
That proved them free.

I   Elderly Lady Crossing on Green

And give her no scouts doing their one good deed
Or sentimental cards to wish her well
During Christmas time or gallstone time—
Because there was a time, she'd like to tell,

She drove a loaded V8 powerglide
And would have run you flat as paint
To make the light before it turned on her,
Make it as she watched you faint

When looking up you saw her bearing down
Eyes locking you between the wheel and dash,
And you either scrambled back where you belonged
Or jaywalked to eternity, blown out like trash

Behind the grease spot where she braked on you. . . .
Never widow, wife, mother, or a bride,
And nothing up ahead she's looking for
But asphalt, the dotted line, the other side,

The way she's done a million times before,
With nothing in her brief to tell you more
Than she's a small tug on the tidal swell
Of her own sustaining notion that she's doing well.

| The Monument

Standing apart yet oddly sequential
In our timed and untimed arrivals, some
Casually late, some impatiently prompt,
But indeed all lining up respectfully,
Just as the signs have said we ought to do,
We watch the elevator dial start up then stop
Then start again, sweeping along its scale
As off ahead near where the line begins
A mother reads aloud from a guidebook
To her children, who yawn and do not listen . . .

As the pulleys to the elevator drone,
Spinning down through the shaft that takes us up,
Till the ornate arrow slows and settles
Over the double doors' subtractive *whoosh*
And lets the crowd that's gone before step off
And shoulder by without a single hint
Why we should take their place, shouldering up,
As now it's our time on the steep ascent,
Where we will push then pause then crowd us through,
Not seeing the symbol but the view.

1   A Note of Thanks

Wallet stolen, so we must end our stay.
Then, while checking out, the wallet reappears
With an unsigned note saying, "Please forgive me;
This is an illness I have fought for years,
And for which you've suffered innocently.
P.S. I hope you haven't phoned about the cards."
I wave the wallet so my wife will see.
Smiling, she hangs up, and smiling she regards
The broad array of others passing by,
Each now special and uniquely understood.
We go back to our unmade room and laugh,
Happily agreeing that the names for "good"
Are not quite adequate and that each combines
Superlatives we but rarely think.
For the next three nights we drink a better wine.
And every day we go back through to check
The shops, buying what before had cost too much,
As if now Christmas and birthdays were planned
Years in advance. We watch others and are touched
To see how their faces are a dead-panned
Generality, holding close
The wishes and desires by which we all are gripped.
All charities seem practical to us,
All waiters deserving of a bigger tip.
And, though we counter such an urge,
We start to think we'd like to meet the thief,
To shake the hand of self-reforming courage
That somehow censored a former disbelief.

Then we are home and leafing through the bills
Sent us from an unknown world of pleasure;
One of us likes cheap perfume; the other thrills
Over shoes, fedoras, expensive dinners;
There are massage parlors and videos,

Magazines, sunglasses, pharmaceuticals,
Long-distance calls, a host of curios,
Gallons of booze. . . . Only now we make our call.
But then, on hold, we go on sifting through
The mail till turning up a postcard view
Of our hotel. Flipping it and drawing blanks,
We read, "So much enjoyed my stay with you
I thought I ought to jot a note of thanks."

Stillness

Returning to the spent house its emptiness,
Letting its windows go as they have gone,
Opened from one abandonment to another,
To the yard grown wildly immeasurable
In the greens, reds, yellows, and browns
Of a fall that comes like someone pausing
Between remembering a name and speaking
The long recollection that a name unfolds . . .

Or, leaving the sagging doors ajar,
Stuck in disagreement with their hinges
And forever met halfway between
Closing on those who left for good
And opening to the abandoned, useless
Ways our going away made of them . . .

Returning to these stubborn, collapsing facts
That are not themselves but always us,
The ones who took their meals and slept upstairs,
There where no stairs can lead us now,
There where the quiet things said before sleep
Are forever truly quiet . . . returning
As if to someone else's carefulness,
We now take down by board and nail
All we ever loved and drove into place.

The Wedding Stop

The walls were thin, and when he left
To dig out something in the trunk
She heard the TV from one side,
While on the other voices rose—
Children complaining, someone explaining.

Later, she watched her husband's face relax
Into a loosened version of himself,
Slack jaw against one arm, face turned,
As where he slept he deepened alone.
So she let the day replay itself,
The white of her continuous day,
With its music, smiles, and flowers.

And then there was the white-noise fan
Loud in the vent above her head
And the intervals of something like crying,
Till she thought about her parents' house,
The outside cold lengthening their hall . . .
There was the crying somewhere, the fan,
Her husband's breathing. Then she slept.

In the morning, loud pipes and voices,
So she eased out, palms cautioning the door,
Where she stepped backwards, watching her husband sleep.
Then she was by herself and got a look . . .
A woman off a ways, shadowed in her door,
Drawn mouth, three children standing back of her.
Then all of them were in their jumbled car,
With its smeared windows and fitful engine,
Till the balding man behind the wheel
Found reverse, and the car lurched backwards
Through its blue exhaust. And still she was glad.

| A Box of Leaves

Collected from childhood's high October,
And sealed under the milky paraffin
Almost forever as they were,
These reds, browns, and yellows, not of a season
But of a season's end, are our reminders
Of a simplicity we never tire
Of telling: that we are lost among ourselves;
Like Dante's suicides, the slightest gust
Tears us from our proper stems to scuttle
In a crowd of bent and drying ironies.
We say no two are ever quite the same
Yet never see that two as different,
Except, perhaps, in how, having lasted
For a long time, such category
May loosen grip, widening from sight.
"Leaves," we say, and generalize each leaf away
In a summary of qualities
Changeable as a season's changing weather.
Waxed, labeled, and carefully put from sight,
These wait alone, safely past their calendar;
Frail and familiar, foreign and lovely,
Not as themselves but as their others.

| The Water Slide along the Beach

It is someone's mimicry, the clockworks
Of wave and tide and shifting weather,
Which, when filled and turned on, makes rhythmical
The textured and turquoised edge of our stilled gulf.

Ages ten and seven, they beg to go.
And so we take them, swayed backs, taut bellies
Poking forward like impudence.
They are brown enough to be ripe or cooked . . .

And symmetrical as the conchs they find,
Always with the same exclamations,
The small empty shells they see as beautiful
Because they echo the one who listens.

It is the blood's clichéd continuum,
Traveling from ear to shell to ear again,
That reassures them of their small full seas,
The long grays and blues that wait ahead for them,

The tides that will rise for their departures
Or that will drop, leaving their hulls mired and leaning . . .
And promised vessels passing out of sight
Topping the horizon, where, briefly magnified,

They disappear beyond the wavy plane
Of humane endurance, in which we think
The gulls cry with almost human voices,
Think the stark similes of looking out.

The ships depart. Flags fade. The ships go down,
Down the round that even children know about,
Where China is not reached by pick or shovel,
Only where the lens quits and the eye blinks shut.

Now our nut-brown pair is at the top.
They are waving. We wave encouragement.
Racing down, they bounce, spin, and scream laughter.
Helped out, their wet hands leave wide prints; they drip,

Wipe noses, rush off, demanding that we watch.
     —As if those most powerful ever
Let us drop our eyes from where they see us
Magnified, topping their horizons.

Baseball

About the time I got my first baseman's mitt
I heard that Dizzy Dean was sacked
Because he made a dirty comment
Over the air. Camera zoomed and locked
On a young couple kissing, something slipped
With Dizzy, who then made the call:
"He kisses her on every strike,
And she kisses him on the balls."

In a century banked with guilt and doubt
Sometimes the telling moments come
As inadvertently as Dizzy's joke,
Like Hitler's code before Coventry was bombed,
Or Valéry's remark about Descartes,
"I sometimes think, therefore I sometimes am."

| Flying at Night

Each city is a solitary reef,
Brightening under a phosphorescent tide
At once astringent and invisible.
Lights pulse their distances in strings,
Either purling out to a wider dark
Or squaring a downtown's grid to imitate
The world's steep longitudes, its latitudes.
Sometimes a single car glides down a street,
Its headlights' two white cones tunneling,
And only lighting where the driver has
Already turned. How strange it is to see
The empowered light following that way.
Suddenly the radio erupts
With weather, times, and late advisories.
A voice enumerates; the engine drones.

Then you are out of range for radios
And following an arbitrary line
Across a landscape with its unplanned lights
By which no one can navigate and where
The darkest ridges rise invisibly.
And should the engine stop, there is this joke:
You cannot tell which dark beneath will be
A forest, ridge, or field, so just before
You're down, cut on the landing light,
Then if you don't like what you see, cut it off.
There is that joke . . . which only gets
Its laughter in daylight and on the ground.

For now, the small plane's red interior
Of night lights, maps, and instruments
Powers through two kinds of dark—cities
That sometimes wake and sometimes are asleep,
And overhead an older population,

Orion, Andromeda, Perseus . . .
Who with their dippers, the lion, bull, and fish
Arrange our darkened ways for out and back,
Most accurately and uncaringly so,
As sometimes to one side the local moon
Pulls up and pales us with its used light,
Under which we go, plying our lost and found.

| Letter for the End

for Howard Nemerov

Who would want to become his admirers?
Still, he was so gracious at the end
It was our sorrow that he talked away
In his genial Job-like manner.

For years he cataloged our likenesses,
Through the leaf-spent acids of seasons
Raked and burned or rotting implosively,
Their figures turned like witnesses

To a proof inside the indelible
Cold, tightening each fall toward winter.
And then there were the snows, whose white chaos
Was as pure as unintelligible,

For the sleepless boy, or the waking man
Discovering once more he only watched
The beautiful despairing joke repeat . . .
Where raked leaves ever took their trees again.

Anything to say to make things better,
Of how the random seeds inscribed their end
By dying upward into power.
Knowing this, for years he wrote his letter.

I Old Declaratives

No calculation holds the miles endured.
Perhaps that's why some families seem stunned,
Waiting in stations or by the tracks,
Patting their pockets to check for tickets,
Their small clasped bags almost identical . . .
As are the ways they have paid, paid the same
Fare to the same repeating agent,
Then pressed themselves in bunches through drawn doors,
Reading the smudged signs identifying seats
Where, adjusting and looking out ahead
Or back, they nod, and sometimes sleep.

Outside, the fields drift by like a promise,
To the immigrant believing seasons change
Predictably, that what he plants will rise
In fairness to the hours he has worked.
And next, the landscape interrupts itself.
No one knew the towns could grow so tired.
The chimneys are silent flutes; each window's X'd.
Walking off the job, thousands must have stumped
Through the sludge, junk, and the bent, sighing grass
Where the tracks, however parallel,
Narrowed the same way either way.

Were there a guidebook, it would say
To take another route; it would advise
A trip into the mountains where the view
Adjusts itself, where trees have overgrown
The mine shaft's rails and the tunnel's dark descent.
Or else it would suggest the ocean's gray
Reflexive tides that wash their limits up
From underneath, where limits never hold.
And in that same guidebook, perhaps there is

A page torn out, some missing numbers
That will never say what slips past now . . .

Empty streets, dead yards, and tumbled houses,
The blank windows of red brick factories
Where some once marched or were let go.
And other replicas that become us—
A small girl's doll, weed-sunken swings,
The way the closed hotel's cracked masonry
Confirms its long abandonment . . .
Or, here, now, suddenly a low salt marsh
That duplicates the reddening sky,
Where three mute gulls have landed for the night
And step together, step darkly red together.

Cousins, Brothers, Sisters

When I was five and said I'd seen an angel,
They said it was the Phantom waiting for me
Because I rivaled him in ugliness.
Jealous, he was hiding in the angle

Of the shadow of my bedroom door;
Or he was standing in the upstairs hall,
Patient, silent, and invisible
To anyone he was waiting for.

That summer every night was filled with losses.
When I was sent upstairs alone to bed,
I stared on vacancies—long shadowed halls
With doors ajar, dark windows, distant voices.

Now that I've seen death's ugliness,
Dyeing us in the many shades he takes,
I know I watched in awe, that sleep came on
From dark to darker emptiness,

While the voices down the stairs or up the hall
Talked on awhile, then paused, then stopped,
As the others too took their darkened beds
And the house unfolded upward from us all.

| Miss Lucy

First day each fall she lectured
On William of Ockham—who he was,
How wrong he was . . . and always would remain.
Then, warning they'd never understand,
She made them memorize Augustine's lines,
Each of them embarrassed to recite—that
"They begin to depart who begin to love.
Many there are who depart without knowing it."

For the betterment of style, there were
Shakespeare's kings, Lycidas, and Wordsworth's Lucy,
Then the Prayer of Humble Access, which she scrawled
Across the board and made them copy,
"We do not presume," they all scrawled back . . .
Till they copied, cribbed, dozed, skipped, and muddled
Through their year with her, their senior year,
As she reminded them, all year.

They'd seen her clothes in black and white movies.
That much they knew, that and her shoes
Looked like miniature pilings. Shadowing
The hall ahead, she marched, arms counterpoised,
As though she'd joined the Royal Navy.
Six feet, high forehead, thin hair on top,
She had a man's falsetto voice by which
All points of view were torqued third person.

"Now class," she once began, "Miss Lucy
Cannot be with you for the game tonight;
You'll have to ride your busses there and back
Without her. Remember who you are,
As Miss Lucy will have you in mind.
She will be stationed by her radio

Monitoring your game. Miss Lucy is
A strong athletic supporter."

That time they laughed out loud,
Though years later what they recalled
Was not the game's score but how her eyes
Scanned back and forth, slicing the room,
Before she asked them what "saccadic" meant,
Then wrote it on the board, scanned them again
And, turning from their reddened hush, printed
"Scotoma." Did they know what that word meant?

| Blood

Known for its repertory lineages
By which we generalize the who and what,
And for the figures that we make of it,
Bloodline, bloodlust . . . it runs between
The spent asphyxiated blues
Of time and work and that bright filigree
Through which the impounding heart pumps back
Our reddened and ventilated lives—
As if among the wind's announcing leaves
That dryly say the world's deciduous,
We breathed a lasting shape that let us stay.

Scripted in a secret and minute hand
That writes itself and signs its origins
In unrepeated blues and reds,
The blood holds to its systole and diastole,
Flooding and circling rawly on
As rhythmic tides reduplicate their shores,
As opened wounds edge inward, welling,
Fresh surfacing and taken by the air . . .
Till drying to a lake-bed crust of drought,
There where the healing scab prevents the scar,
Blood surfaces our dust, and something more,
The potent changing earth of us.

Great Thoughts and Noble Feelings

A storm, and our window frames the ocean
Like a fluid Turner down the wall.
The waves kick up in a horrible fit
That really would elevate, if someone read

Aloud something Gothic and about graveyards.
And each ecstatic wave's a dying beauty
Splayed out on the sand and bubbling
Better than Lizzie Siddal as Ophelia.

For in between, there's drink, with which we stretch out
Under the long twilight the clouds impose,
Like some great brooding revelation, stalled
Above the daily grind and bubble.

Linked backward to the shore by telephone,
Cable, the mail, newspapers, magazines,
We look into the rich and recondite
Storm, but think our condominium.

This is what the masters meant to teach us,
A sovereignty of sorts, somewhere between
What the decorator's done to everyday,
Inside the atelier we vacuum up,

And what the storm outside does by itself;
Though the spark leap, the longing rise like dough,
We know we are alone, where the ocean's wide
Periphery teaches our narrow passage.

| New Territory

Taking a walk on her first retirement day,
She stopped to watch two starlings glinting
As they circled up then down, widened then closed,
Dogfighting some twenty feet above
Around a spot no one else could see;
Spiraling as they rode two helices
Built in the air, as in their heads,
Which hammered whenever they came close.
Then the one knocked the other down,
Made a strafing run, climbed and stalled
Into a wingover and came back down,
Tines out, landing on the wounded bird
And locking his talons on one leg.

She had not moved from where she stopped.
But now the birds were still, except the one
Who held the other cranked his idiot head
Over the wing, broken open like a fan.
Then the one was gone and the broken one left,
Tossed out like a life raft on the grass—
And she deciding what it was she'd do,
Till the chorus rose and bombing runs began,
Starlings out of every corner of the yard
Angling in over the grounded bird,
Beak here and talon there, and blood . . . till she swore
She'd poison the seed then take the feeders down,
As she turned a different way for home.

The Taking Down

Ever since the seriously ill were sent away,
The sounds, smells, even the lights have changed;
These days the doctors in the valley
Export their help up to our hospital,
Where rarely anyone walks the corridors,
Now lengthened by their emptiness,
Much the way the parking lots outside
Wait like hugely widened game boards,
Especially during the holidays,
When looking out one thinks of visitors.

After Christmas and before New Year's,
The artificial Christmas tree
Is taken down and packed away
"To avoid bad luck," Mrs. Gilbert says.
She and the other volunteers
Sit in the lobby and quietly pack
The coils of wire that, covered with green needles,
Make up the tree's ten feet of branches.
They put the ornaments in smaller boxes,
Each one sealed, labeled, and numbered
So that, next year, they may reverse themselves.

For Mrs. Gilbert, the emptied corridors
And vacant parking lots mean that her wing
Along the back, looking out into the woods
From its rounded nurses' station, lounge, and rooms,
Has cycled the healing roundabout
Of charts, nurses, and starched doctors
Into something barely graspable—
The indefinite December sky
Under which she walked once as a girl,
Hurrying home and looking side to side
Between the houses' deepening porches,

Until she bundled through her own front door,
Lights out and the hall recessively still.
She remembers sitting alone for hours.

This time of year the drive from the hospital
Stretches as the halls on Mrs. Gilbert's wing
Lengthen in the early dark that seems to stall
The backward counting days before New Year's,
After the Christmas visitors have disappeared;
So Mrs. Gilbert busies herself
A little longer in each room,
And takes some added care in overseeing
That the ornaments and artificial tree
Are packed away by proper count,
Boxes numbered and stacked in sequence,
As though matching next year's calendar
By which she will arrange her hall,
Where she walks now, checking every name,
Steering her cart as she has done for five years.

The back wheels swivel as she moves,
Leaning in a push that makes the cart
Seem heavier than it is. Nothing spills.
And her list of names, which rarely changes,
Is on top, printed new each day for her,
As if she were a silent auditor
Hired to hold some closing inventory.
Sometimes her lips move, naming a new patient.
Other times, she pauses at a vacancy
And checks the room, opening the door
And feeling a draft's subtractive touch.

From down the hall Mrs. Henry shouts
Repeatedly, "Take Me Home! Take Me Home!"

Then, offered varieties of drink,
Answers softly, "No thank you, Dear, no thank you."
The cart backed out, the shouting starts again.
Next, Mr. Elmo, who's had a stroke:
"I feel so stupid," he says, shaking his head,
"I'm dead because I'm stupid."
She offers him his cup; he looks away.
Later, when she checks, the cup's still full.

Mrs. Nicholas plays the radio all day.
She cannot use her hands to change the station
But doesn't mind, she says, because
She only wants the human voices going on.
Her friend across the hall, Mrs. Austin,
Has lost the use of her two good hands also.
She leans away, then whispers, "Are you a Christian?"
Surprised, Mrs. Gilbert says, "Yes, yes, I am."
"Then would you scratch my nose?"

Next there is Mrs. Alfred, who asks about
Her husband down the hall, "Is he warm enough?"
"It's Alzheimer's, you know." She likes reports
And always sends a note propped by his cup,
Knowing he will fold the note repeatedly,
Tuck it away, take it out, try to read.

Twice now Mrs. Gilbert's wing has telescoped
As though her head were driven back,
Twice the ceiling, walls, and floor contracted
To a half light, then widened and returned,
As she leaned even farther forward
In her exaggerated push against the cart.
Both times her parents came to mind, grown small

In their clothes as if they shrank from touch,
As if old, though not that yet, tired maybe,
And silent as two sullen absences,
Home late and neither noticing
How cold and dark the house had turned.

Both times her wing tightened to its peep-sight gray,
Mrs. Gilbert paused only briefly,
As though distracted by a name recalled,
Or stalled by something she'd misplaced;
Then, leaning ahead, the back wheels swiveled,
And as she moved her corridor returned to color.

The last room produces Mrs. Clement,
Who propped up in her partially raised bed
Is the best adjusted of them all;
Always with something gracious to say,
She thinks herself a guest in this hotel,
Where she appreciates the service
But occasionally asks for a different room.

With Mrs. Clement and all the rest settled,
And the bronze tinted windows darkening
Toward reflection, Mrs. Gilbert is free
To drive the few blocks home. Sometimes
She stops for something frozen, which she cooks
While listening to the news. After dinner
There are letters, the paper, the news again,
During which Mrs. Gilbert sometimes lists
The names of all the patients on her wing,
Now and for the last five years she's volunteered,
Feeling especially mindful of them now,
Between the two tall holidays,

With all the carols and the visits over
And for the next few quiet days
Little sense of anything ahead.

There's always the artificial tree to pack,
Practical because its needles do not drop,
It will not burn, requires no water,
Is light, and never changes size—
Its ornaments forever adequate . . .
And there are the clocks along the hall,
As round-faced and reassuring
As the water-color seasons painted
On calendars some patients get by mail.

Limited and quirky as these comforts are,
Mrs. Gilbert finds them preferable
To the new clock radios the hospital
Has given as a present to each room,
All of them off-white, with digital faces
Blocked in crude illuminated reds
That reconfigure without changing place.
To Mrs. Gilbert, this collective gift,
A bargain no doubt, plays, in miniature,
All that Times Square, the hotel parties, Big Bands,
On the competing stations—all that these mean—
Summed up, she supposes, by the Times Square crowd itself.

Although she never waits till twelve,
Saying she cannot keep her eyelids up,
Mrs. Gilbert's not too sure how much she sleeps either,
Hearing in the white noise of the vent
Above her bed a rush of overlapping cries;
Only the air, but sometimes when she's tired
She remembers the man she heard about

Who claimed there was a way to play back sounds
Trapped like stilled echoes in rocks, the lava
Of Pompeii, say, the people in confusion,
Calling out and running to no escape.

And sometimes just before she's drifted off,
She hears the static of an old radio,
Her parents' Zenith, audible upstairs
Where she has waited in her bed, half asleep,
Holding out . . . first the background of the crowd,
Then suddenly all one voice and counting down,
As the last few seconds of the year
Widen like drained parentheses.

When she could not sleep without a light,
She too left her radio on for the voices;
She too wrote her husband short careful notes,
Placed beside a photograph or window,
A sentence or a phrase she hoped he'd catch,
Between all the folding and unfolding,
While at home, in bed, there were crosswords to do;
Propped up, her pillows banked a quiet minus,
As she piled their angles into height,
Wondering how deep a sleep could get
Drifting under a few half-completed words.
It was as if she stood dumb in her own name,
Or stilled before the plate glass to a shop
That, lights turned out, darkened and reflecting,
Gave her back a face she'd never seen.

But what she calls the taking down,
The season that she now walks through,
Stretches wide of any one reflection,
Wide even of her bringing water

To the few stalled days remaining
Of the shipped apples, oranges, and pears
Lining the complex sills to every room . . .
And the names, the essential names,
Answer through the hall's suffusing gray
As she feels somehow they always did,
Long before her leaning to the cart's odd wheels,
Or finding in the air's subtractive touch
That each was thirsty and completely recognized.

Balance as Belief

Learning the Bicycle

for Heather

The older children pedal past
Stable as little gyros, spinning hard
To supper, bath, and bed, until at last
We also quit, silent and tired
Beside the darkening yard where trees
Now shadow up instead of down.
Their predictable lengths can only tease
Her as, head lowered, she walks her bike alone
Somewhere between her wanting to ride
And her certainty she will always fall.

Tomorrow, though I will run behind,
Arms out to catch her, she'll tilt then balance wide
Of my reach, till distance makes her small,
Smaller, beyond the place I stop and know
That to teach her I had to follow
And when she learned I had to let her go.

I The Wild Horses

The horses imagined by a boy
Who cannot get himself to sleep
Are grazing so deep within a story
He cannot say what it means to keep
Such things inside and at a distance;
They are a silent governance
He feels but cannot name.
The horses change, and are the same.
They run miles farther than the meadows
In which he sees them run. They have no shadows,
Are unceasing, and they never die.
What he feels when watching them is like a cry
Heard somewhere else, and neither pain
Nor happiness in it, but sustained
Like a long note played in an empty room.
And that is how he waits for sleep, which soon
Takes him deeper than the fastest animal
As he tunnels clockwise in a fall,
The meadows rising through him, then gone
Somewhere above, until alone
He sees the horses turn in one long curve
That rounds them back where nothing moves,
And he knows that they were always blind,
Running from what they heard each time
The wind would shift, running away
Because they could not see their way.

To him, the horses are beautiful and sad;
They are a celebration made
Out of the way they end, begin again,
A morning's bright imperative sustained
Long after dark. They are a walling out
By looking in, what opens when he shuts
His eyes, the body's quiet allegory

By which it knows itself, a story
Told against the body that it cannot see.
The horses run because they're free
And incomplete, while poised somewhere between
The half-light in the hall and what he's seen
Inside, the boy wakes or sleeps, or turns against
His sleep, naming a larger self that rests
Invisibly, yet in sight of what it sees,
Rests without feeling, in the calculated ease
Of someone small, afraid, and fragile,
Alone and looking out, flexed but agile.

| Falling through the Ice

This, one of our oldest tales—
Late winter and the boy who skates
Ahead in darkness, staying out late
With his thin-voiced friends from school who sail
Over the ice till someone calls them home
And now, turned last, the one drops from sight,
Crying for help where the snow's grained white
Sifts over into dark.
                           His parents come;
Men ladder out across the ice,
Shouting when they find the hole, but he is gone
Far down below the reasoned town
Where suddenly the shops close twice
Because he's drifting underneath
A surface where his father's breath
Clouds everything but death.
That's how it happens, muted, brief,
And fittingly cold; we tell it over
To ourselves and to each other
Because it pulls us back again
This side of what no man
Has ever laddered over with a name . . .
A riddle, a story, a children's game.

| The Covined Bird

The story told was how, before
He settled, my father hunted land
He'd never seen and wound up lost.
Walking a creek through uncut woods,
He found a lean-to built against
A bank, door opened, furniture inside,
Nothing else. It was cold, raining,
And getting dark, so he slept there—
Not on the rope bed or in a chair
But on the floor beside a trunk.

Next day, he shot a turkey hen,
"Dishragged her," he said. The bird had flown
Straight down on him; he raised, first shot,
The pellets gutted her midair.
He hung his kill, bleeding its throat,
Then built a fire and plucked it clean,
Saving the smoothest feathers from
What he later called his covined bird.
When I was small and sick for a long time,
He used to spread those feathers on my bed.

He hadn't eaten since he left his camp
The day before. The bird he killed
Was all the game he'd seen, and it
Had flown into his sights as if
Somehow angling home for him.
He'd heard its chalked-wood muttering
Before it flew, had searched for others
It must have called, but there was nothing.
Reluctant in an unknown house,
He cooked outside, but rested near the door,

Then slept a while, feeling himself
Rise and sink like someone breathing water.
Waking, he heard his bird's chalked cries again,
Coming from in the house. He waited;
One ear set to the stilled interior,
The other to the creek etching from sight,
There was no mistake in what he heard.
He stood, walked in, waited, nothing there—
Stepped out, the calling started up.
He eased back in, looked more carefully;

Found nothing again. The place he skipped
Was the trunk, too clearly someone else's,
But that was where he found the thing.
Inside, a boy at least three feet,
Dried to perfection; he'd seen this once
In school and thought nothing of it,
But here was a child age four or so
With wrapping twine sewn in his belly,
Where someone had either stabbed him
Or tried to save him, likely both.

Already middle-aged, a doctor,
He'd seen enough to weather this,
But didn't; settling to the floor,
He stared, then felt himself recede
From that house, the woods, everything.
Then he was back, got up, found a soft
Indentation in the bank and deepened it,
Wrapped the small mummy in his shirt
And buried it under a pile of stones,
A private cairn, but to no reckoning.

Working south from the house and creek,
He climbed up to a logging trail
Then turned due west, following ruts
Now barely visible, but the path
Played out into another uncut wood
So he started back the other way.
Passing where he found the trail, he saw
A trace of smoke angling from the lean-to,
Another hunter, or something else.
He didn't stop to see what followed there

But walked on out to where his trail
Turned to a dirt road that ran downhill
And fed into a blacktop road.
He hitched a ride to the main camp,
Packed his gear, said nothing to his friends,
And drove back home. That was fifty years ago.
He hunted several places then—
Fiery Gizzard, Cold Creek, Dead Tree . . .
Places I've never seen but where
I know you're better lost than caught.

He said that we were given back to him
For what he killed along that creek
And in the house; it was a rush of air
That's only heard inside a hollow place,
Something he knew but hadn't met,
As if he'd slept inside that house before
Moving familiarly, touching his way
Between two kinds of sleep, the one
Deep and generous, the other waiting
Like a fear born long before its name.

I Water

How can we own a thing that travels
Constantly, evaporates, clouds over,
Rains back and pools,
                    or else sinks,
Each fold or fault distorting its movement
In ways no sense of gravity predicts?
And how can we know the lateral habits
Of water, an immigrant who cannot
Settle anywhere, but circles over
Landscapes, erodes every border,
Edges shorelines of immeasurable sand.

Etched banks can channel it,
The current cutting deeper down,
Driving itself from underneath,
No longer water then but the force
Of gravity gathering its weight.
A watershed deflects the rain,
Or water table drops from use,
The downhill graduals of streams,
Spring floods and overflowing dams—
All tributaries feeding down
Into one long revisionary river
That curls against itself as if
The only way to move ahead
Was by deflecting back,
Like a language that explains itself,
A story told,
                    this time about water.

I   The Hand-me-down

His father's clothes embarrass him
Like the five o'clock shadow that
Darkens his smile when he comes home
Carrying the bundled shirts and hat

Sent him as if to ask, "Where were you?"
They lump the whole event into
A wrinkled emptiness that shapes
Like rounded shoulders; someone waits

Ceremonious and still inside
Those folded sleeves, once opened wide.
Daphnis, Persephone, Adonis,
Atthis, Orpheus—all come to this:

The dying sex that promises return
Like spring, cut flowers, is a wreath that burns
As brightly as it disappears
Around its empty center.

Knowing there is no out, he calls
Things in, homing an animal
Scared of itself because it dies
Momently back into familiar eyes.

All mourning is inheritance,
Brief similarities and distance
In the very place he stands
Broken by what reaches his hand.

| The Name

With an easiness we almost learn . . .
Like the isolated shadow of a palm
Or variegated light by which a fern
Casts the lattice of its green calm—
Two workers lift in place a new fountain
For the courtyard in the starched hotel
Where, retired, my parents visited and remained.
Now, there's little here of them to tell,
Except that they were happy spending
Their days in shops, or walking the battery
When evenings cast outlines of the ending
They treated with such baroque finality.
Old clothes outgrew them, though their profiles changed
As imperceptibly as the courtyard
Where, year after year, they still arranged
Small gatherings and monitored
Their guests like two strict preservationists.

For years they did the ordinary thing—
The suburbs in a haze, high hedge and smoke
From cigarettes and grill, bluffed twinings
Overhead, rising beyond the jokes,
Choked laughter, and descending ice
Poured from lilting pitchers . . . premium gin
Precise as medicine.
                    And twice,
Promotion or the market up—some win—
The two of them waltzed across the patio
Laughing, we children laughing, not knowing why,
As the afternoon turned evening like a slow
Fade-out under a canvas sky.

There was a game we played in which
One child held a flashlight and one a mirror,
Attacker and attacked, the switch
Coming when, angled just right, the mirror
Blinded back, and then the game reversed.
I think our parents played that way,
But differently, more slowly, and with words.
It was their means for setting things to stay,
Not out of differences or change
But somehow from the names they played
Back to one point—each view exchanged.

What brings me to this hotel now
Is a kind of stalled curiosity
Opening out the way a pattern goes
From holding its geometry
To something wider.
                        Crisp habits raise
Their own squared world, but lack
The final fact, when every gaze
Becomes the other view. The child
Looks up and back, then looks ahead
Beyond his own eroding ground, wild
As a nightmare's cranking landscape of the dead,
Where he calls the names he knows but no one wakes.
There water is the only constancy;
It fills headlong whatever way it takes,
Channeling a deep redundancy
As it steadies where its banks divide
Wider with floods, higher with drought.
For me that landscape was the side
Of a failing wall, a fountain's spout
Widening as I listened to regret

Coiling and uncoiling like a chain
Linking everything it touched. It let
Me stand once, balanced like a name,
Realizing that the water fell by rising,
And that what it brought and took away were the same.

To Be Sung on the Fourth of July

We come to this country
By every roundabout,
With hunger like a startled face
And passports folding doubt,

With leaving home as commonplace
As children waking clear,
And hopeful as a fishline cast
Deep from the harbor's pier

To the idea of a country,
The garden and the name,
And a government by language,
Called the New Jerusalem,

Where the trees have figured upward
As much as shadowed down;
And when we stood beneath them
We hugely looked around,

Because our gift is figures
That turn along our thought,
The apple, rock, and water,
The ram suddenly caught—

A country of inheritors
Who only learn of late,
Who set their eyes as blankly
As their livestock stand and wait,

There where the markets bicker
Till the bell has rung them home,
There where Chicago bargains
The wheat crop for a loan,

Wait like the black lake barges
That punctuate a course
Or linger in ellipsis
Between the yawning shores . . .

And then that huge interior
That always seems the same,
Abandoned wells, neglected fields,
And immigrants who came

Mapping the land they traveled for,
Stayed, worked a while, then died,
Or moved to cities where
They also worked and died

As, settlers who burned and built
And surveyed every line,
We timbered, plowed, and harvested
To songs in three-four time.

Our figures are like fireworks,
And water turned to fire;
In Cleveland or Chicago
The people never tire

Of the ballads of an innocence
That would not be dissolved,
But burned the witch and stuck like tar . . .
To the first citizen ever saved.

And though at times in chorus,
The music almost right,
We sing away the darkness
That makes a window bright,

In fact we're born too lucky
To see a street's neglect,
For the years have pushed us next to
An unalike Elect—

Who say the lost are with us
The way our backs go bad
Or eyes require new glasses
To peer into what's sad,

Which occupies the TV set
And functions by contrast,
Because well-being needs a grief
To make the feeling last.

Dr. Williams' Garden

for Paul Mariani

A city, a mountain, a river,
And somewhere else a garden snake
Mildly frightening to the child
Who steps across its length before
It disappears into the grass—

The snake recedes in memory
The way the child explains what he has seen,
Detail distancing detail until
The snake cannot return but must become
Another city, mountain, river;
And somewhere else the child has grown
Into a man who cannot say
What he has seen without his losing it.

And so he says it thing by thing,
Knowing that the words will leave him
Bankrupt beyond all tragedy,
As he stands beside a waterfall
Remembering the lusty heart
Of a fetus lost, or the sick heart
Of the young father who looked at him
And, buttoning his shirt, said nothing—.
A city, a mountain, a river
And everything still left to do
By a man whose feet go so unevenly
Over such uneven grass and accident,
That love must be a waterfall
Beside which good balance is belief.

| Memorial Day

From shade to shade our neighbor mows
His civic way through the flexed spring grass,
Thick in its resurgent category
Of green, and widening from the eye.

He passes back and forth as if
Heard from a swing or hammock where
Someone almost asleep is letting
His motion sway the sound of things

Through an easy grazing pendulum
By which his season clocks itself . . .
While the grass is cut and kept from bearing seed
And the man will purchase what he needs

Of green, admixture bagged and weighed
Of every neighbor and his neighborhood,
Till it germinates from his scything wrist,
Who sews brief shadows, and in shadow rests.

The Actuarial Wife

for Patty

About their chances for divorce,
She says, "Slim—
Because the one who leaves
Will have to take the children."

About their children,
She says,
"We should have waited until
They were older to have them."

But most about her husband's smoking.
He's fifty now, and, taking stock
Of all they have, she stands outside
The blue haze through which he angles down
Into his favorite easy chair
Like an accurate punt, perfect hang time,
To read the morning paper over coffee
And start another pack of Luckies, stubbed
Emphatically, like punctuation marks
Down through an urgent argument.
She clarifies their options for retirement:
"Darling, if one of us dies,
I'm going to live in Paris."

| Playing by Ear

Plunking the keys until sent out
To plunk anything that didn't resonate,
So, playing the sticks against a fence
And tremoring garbage cans with rocks . . .
Later, reaching the Zenith's off-on-
volume-switch, which twisted full circle,
Tubes warming, till the music dopplered
Like a headlong freight that didn't pass
And I was ushered out again . . .
And what I learned was how things sound,
And that they sound so differently.

We had a mockingbird who came back year
After year, possessive, inventive,
Self-distancing inside his tree,
Where he built medleys from other voices—
Not like that corny radio star,
The Whistler, whose melody and pitch
Dried on his lips with selling manuals
So you could whistle after.
                              For him,
You were a silence.
                              But for the small fierce bird
Others were a threat he warned away
By mimicry. You heard yourself,
And knew to be afraid.
                              And that is how
You play by ear, self-separating,
Like allegory from the other side,
Where the distance in a mimicked world
Is reason enough to make things hide.

| Crosswords

Devoted to the compost pile,
She carried back their coffee grounds,
Odd table scraps the dog refused,
Rinds, cores, eggshells, old newspapers,
Until he said his will required
An open-casket funeral
To guarantee she'd bury him.

And when he died the garden ran
To weeds, wealthy under her homely
Ministrations wearing out the plot
She turned by years against more years,
Feeding her well-fed encumbrances—
Children, grandchildren, even pets
Brought home to pee, scratch, and chew the furniture.

At night she watched the news alone,
Then worked the crosswords into sleep;
Once she dreamed he spoke, praising their years,
And she saw small children standing still,
Waiting for the two of them to move.
But when she reached, it all was gone
Into a weather washed from sight

By a blue haze and blank dispersal
Vaster than any amplitude
The heart sounds out of its bruised range;
Leaves winked the sun, and a shallow light
Washed under trees as if the tide
Of their green mass curled over her
Saying, "The only thing you loved was change."

I Late Days

Late light across a side porch where
Two people play canasta—laugh,
Shuffle, talk, then deal the decks and stare
As if the cards, played out, will graph
Their afternoon, their working out
A private rhetoric, some stance
Each pauses over like a bet
Without debate, a preference
That carries them forward yet narrows
As the house bulks white against its shadow.

And as they stall above their game
Their laughing tears among the trees,
Echoing distances with names
That drift alone among the leaves
As they loosen wildly but color down,
Graceful in the quilting avenues
That settle as the season drowns
Along the ground, until the shade subdues
Their laughter, loosening like a weight
That drops where now they touch and hesitate.

1 Good-bye

for John and Laura

Whatever we are, we're torn like strips
Of cloth, and knotted together against
A wind whose changes are our directions
Read backwards, tugging away from where,
Facing, we watch ourselves fluttering home
From what the eye's transparency engulfs—
All we ever thought, because what we thought
Is there, *is* given, yet leads us back,
Though not to one place but to one starting out.
This is good-bye; this breaks the heart.

Because we are a knot that stops itself,
A thing that holds the way a seed
Carried by air beyond its origin
Catches and swells till its economy
Enfolds another starting out,
We are a script within a later script,
Written for light, air, earth, and water
In a place made out of openness.
We make it our common place,
Our origin all over again.

Look deeper through that place and watch
The leaf unfolding as the root unfolds,
Till later, the green, outreaching limbs
Fan beneath a sky rounding from sight
As if each branch's shade were something whole,
Growing to every part. No line divides;
Leaf, limb, and seed—the trunk that holds
Such branching thought up green against
Our circumfused first questioning,
This is our first analogy.

Below the trunk, the root takes hold,
Thickens, and burrows out of sight,
A blank albino thirsting downward,
Like our Fall again, self-separating
And hungry as our nakedness.
Whatever leaf we took to cover that
Turned into sickness and to death—
A mother's pain, and food by sweat
Out of a grudging field whose furrows
Approximate the way we end.

Good-bye waved out our generation
Through a jungle's underbrush; limbs broke
With boys stiffened against the thing
They saw when shaving, themselves reversed,
Like fathers, framed in a bristled force
That felt like want. They never wanted what
Those fathers meant, night watches where
The enemy was every breathing leaf,
A rhetoric of sudden silences,
And opposites who aimed good-bye.

My daughter bleeds because good-bye
Has turned her so, her temperament
Rebelling against a self-betraying
Innocence in which she is caught,
Asking, who asked for this? Her mother splits
With telling why, so many ways—
The cramp that swells and also splits
Into another openness,
Crying with hunger. Cries muffled
Like a covered seed the heart enfolds.

It is the comic's clipped delivery,
Good-bye . . . his joke shut down
On someone tagged before first base.
Deadpan and perfect timing, he leads
Us through the incongruities
Of fat, stingy, dumb. The fat laugh loudest.
The lights turned down to anonymity,
We follow what is done to others—
Laughing, "We are not you; we are not like you
But are ourselves," until the laughter dies.

Good-bye is a child's clean slate on which
Someone must write his name repeatedly,
Or else he cannot free himself
From a room in which the walls breathe
Like a resting animal, or whale
That vomits up a god's scared messenger,
Caught between the words he's made to say
And his terror over saying them,
His language like a desert wind, audible
Against the tree, tower, or town that resists.

And it is like our other self
Hung threadbare on a tree to suffocate.
Our language breathes him back again;
But no matter how we try, the story
Recoils into its first recorded facts,
Our telling it sometimes as predatory
As any time we ever killed
And made it true. We eat and drink
Good-bye collectively, and call
It love by a raveling tale.

Good-bye is the beginning that
We never knew, the fruit at once ripe
And green, torn mother with her kneading child.
It is a landscape we are homesick for
But have never seen, a place projected
Out of need. We tear plain cloth,
Tie knots, and watch the wind ribbon us back.
Myth, song, a fruitful place to pause . . .
We arrive out of our terrible freedom
Which kills and loves us like a starving mother.

The Lake House

They water-ski over whitecaps
The wind tops up on a man-made lake
Outside Atlanta.
                The water widens
Green to blue where their slaloms sculpt
Brief arcs around peninsulas
Jutting out of red-banked Georgia.
It's 1969. She salutes
Left-handed, shading her eyes,
Watching successive skiers pass
And diminish where their wakes fan out;
Then the sun brightens, fixed things waver,
So she turns from her pier and walks into
The cool of a stone summer house.
The skiers crisscross back and forth,
Arms straightened to the ski rope's tug,
Tanned bodies angling back through curve
After curve, rhythmical, as if
Some gradual was silently towing them
Across a plain balanced between
Two bells,
             the earth cupped upward,
The sky cupped down,
                 and water deepening
Blue into blue beyond focus.

Inside, the house stills everything,
Its rooms a series of silences
Arranging furniture, each with
Its view, the lake, a picture window
Squaring another set of silences—
Skiers rounding beyond the window's frame,
Elliptic where they cut high rooster tails
Repeated like a child's toy that's wound,

Released, then wound again.
In the last room down the hall a boy's things
Stand boxed, dated years ago.

                      He's flying now
Over Southeast Asia; what's left behind
Are flags, biplanes, a train, bright cars,
And on the ceiling

                stars arranged
In tiny constellations, Serpens,
Perseus, Andromeda, Orion . . .
Placed in a circle so, "Lights Out,"
He could lie on his back and navigate
Across a ceiling as close and clear
As the luminous face of his father's watch,
His father gone, flying for Nimitz
And Bull Halsey.

                That ceiling never altered;
Its bright particulars were fixed points of
A boy's departure, small geometries
Set wide against his fear of sleep.

At school he heard the Japanese
Stretched prisoners on bamboo shoots
Then walked away, indelicate
To hear the screams, as the green shafts
Drove up in dark, reaching for light
Till the ground was still and green again.
And then Hiroshima, Nagasaki.
But nothing changed. No one returned.
Beside the cracked, concrete highway to town,
Stone Mountain's half-completed generals
Rode south with Lee, as if the next few steps
Might break them free of their locked origin.
Weekends, the Piedmont Driving Club . . .

Golf, tennis, the pool, or Fox Theater,
And Peachtree Street's dogwoods in bloom—
Then Ponce de Leon Avenue
Unraveling late light through pines,
Curving into 1969
When he's not thought of bamboo shoots
For years, or needed stars fixed overhead
To get to sleep, his missing father
Stalled in shallow spirals,
Wings angling a glide path home
But his Corsair never "touching down."

This is a story about a story,
Two times at once because a woman
Opens her lake house for the summer;
Moving from room to room, she cleans
Windows, gauging her strict horizon
As it distends outside on water,
A litany of successive nows
In which her son and husband stand,
Both young, and thus their lives
Going separately at once, as they
Angle away, two large, high-noon shadows
That never meet.
                   She almost prays,
Saying, "If only for a moment,
Let my thinking take the place
Of their two absences so that
I see them here again, the water
Buoying their energetic waves
As, banking, they ski beyond this lake
Into one bright, continuous curve
Back home, where they dwell again in me."

Their dwelling hollows every room.
Turning, she thinks the sunlight's best
For plants in corners, there urging her ferns
And dieffenbachia up to the clean,
Cool edges of her windowsills
That let onto the water's glaze.
Outside, the lake steadies the day.
Inside, her gaze extends to where
The sky and water meet, a draftsman's line,
The water rising into its opposite.

One opposite confers another.
Sometimes she starts half-stunned because
The skiers lean through curves the way
Her son has learned to shoulder his plane.
She wonders if someway he thinks
He'll find his father out ahead
Caught in one last aerobatic roll
Beneath a Zero tailing him
Like a tireless predatory bird
He cannot see because the sun's
Behind the plane, only a glint
Above before it fires on him
Still in his roll, arching upward
But looking down, two waiting cups,
Two blues identical and wide
Of thought.
                      There's nothing up or down,
As their son, one wing away, alert,
Tightens into his own high-speed shedding
That is terror banking into itself.
She is dusting but, seeing this,
Hunches till her hands let go,
Then stares because she's dropped a glass

Between her feet, its tiny fragments
Scattered in a soft blue constellation
Patterning the place she stands, uncertain
What she was doing, or what she will do.
Beyond the house, only the light shatters
Where the wind cuts up the lake like glass
Reflecting upward in a thousand pieces.

I Rio

This down by which we go runs like
One thought. Great river barges widen it
Into a traffic silent and slow
As any growth that took a body
To its maturity or quiet end.
With evening, cool running lights
Practice direction but never change,
Two ways to go but only one leads out.
For some, the river's merciless and pure
As an upland thawing stream
Where gravity is headlong and heedless,
Until there's nothing bent, only what bends;
For others, it is a mother slow and sorrowful
Murmuring her missing children's names,
Names lost like objects dropped, sedimented,
Or like trapped gestures, articulate and bright
On a silted bed that never settles.

Each tide an estuary toward the moon,
The moon a rounding back into its tide,
The lost idea imagines us all new again . . .
Until its tributaries widen to
One current where a river cuts
Its way, less narrow as it goes,
And the last of it never closing off
But something like the mother fish
Whose mouth collects her young, then lets them out again,
As if she spoke her children into life.

Some stories have no end but tell us out
Into an opening where, turning, we
Begin repeatedly, listening
As our telling takes away and gives
Us all we ever had, missed, believed.

Having and not having is how we go,
Like hope beyond reason . . . some lost thing found
Become a gift because we had forgotten
Where it was, a gift out of
Two ownerships, a rich recovery.

Too long at sea, too little time on shore,
Glass raised and nothing left to raise
Except the silent ways the people found
To join and separate . . . handshake, half-wave
From the Bondé on the viaduct . . .
What I recall was comical and cruel,
The dirt and wealth of Rio during Carnival—
Blown papers kiting up, the smog,
Crisp sails of ocean-going racers
Singling in from the Cape Town Race.

Along the streets impromptu bands
Arranged themselves, blared, settled, marched,
Gradually building a following;
The traffic stopped, police and drivers
Studying the masks that nodded past them
Down one long contrapuntal avenue
Wide as a city block and full
Of bright, gaudy, exaggerated faces.

High laughter is a cry sustained,
And painted masks are many cries at once
When women dance their own round mobile,
Balancing their grinning lamentations.
But on a terrace above the bay,
Two people slipped into a samba,
And nothing steadied where they stepped;
The music was anatomy

Bodied forth in easy choruses
Until they moved so strictly opposite
They rounded everything, yet gazed
Into some middle ground that dulled their eyes.
They danced before the rest, earlier
And balancing against the bay
As the half-cocked moon bled everything . . .
The water, sand, Avenida Atlántica,
Even the dirt-pathed *favelas*
That bunched in quiet distances,
Almost toppling, as pricked from hillsides
With packing crates, odd boards, old signs,
They held the world to one story—
Up close, few lights, mostly the moon bland on
Corrugated roofs, by day too hot to touch
But now cool and subdued as those who slept
Or sat in doors to get a breeze
Round corners where small children played
Near naked bulbs that pocketed the dark.
The smallest of them wore no clothes
And at the farthest reaches of the light
Their thin brown arms became invisible,
Fey as the grass fires that drove them to the coast,
Or as the tiny water organisms
That waited for their lives like thirst.

I watched the two who danced against the bay,
And knew that their distracted steps
Took them past the limits of the little towns
From which so many came, took everything
Beyond the scale of just endurance,
To where deserted animals will turn,
Circling out of the way, or people

Living on the street will sleep coiled
As if they meant to wake running;
While beauty was the brief indifference
Of a dance, which I could only watch,
Thinking how strange it was to name
A river for a time, for explorers,
Not knowing where they were but when,
To say, Rio de Janeiro,
Naming departure for return—
Balancing a city that, bulldozing down
And scaffolding up the same cramped needs,
Was as angular and thin along the coast
As any new-world history . . .
While Guanabara Bay curved back
Into an arc of crowded avenues
That channeled inland like so many fingers
Pushed through a Carnival in which
Each dressed as someone else and all
Found their way a making way dividing where
They danced, crowded and anonymous
As the *movimento* of their millions . . .
Each empty hand a plucking down;
But one by one so many lifting up.

| A Winter's Tale

for Ian

Silent and small in your wet sleep,
You grew to the traveler's tale
We made of you so we could keep
You safe in our vague pastoral,

And silent when the doctors tugged
Heels up your body free of its
Deep habitat, shoulders shrugged
Against the cold air's continent

We made you take for breathing.
Ian, your birth was my close land
Turned green, the stone rolled back for leaving,
My father dead and you returned.

1 | The Depression, the War, and Gypsy Rose Lee

H. L. Mencken called me an ecdysiast. I have also been described
as deciduous. The French call me a deshabilleuse.
In less refined circles
I'm known as a strip teaser.
—Gypsy Rose Lee

In a photograph now left to me
Two people lock their arms and pose;
Leaning against a car's black, boxy side,
Cigarettes held out, eyes squinting,
My parents smile into the sun,
So close their white clothes blur
Into one image.
     It's 1938;
Most things are cheap and unaffordable,
The war ahead with money to spend
And nothing to buy, ready as any
         substitute
To draft people from part-time jobs
To a full-time hitch,
       and anonymous
As orders through the mail,
        or targets
That synchronize with calendars
And newsreels ticking black and white.

Soon things will be standardized,
The prefab buildings, starched uniforms,
Haircuts, and requisitioned tires,
Even the Big Band Sound on radios
Whose dials illuminate the stilled faces
Of those listening for news between
Two coasts darkened against attack.

Traveling west at forty-five,
My parents will drive at night to duck the heat
And save the rationed, recapped tires
That peel their tread regardless what.

Promises.
                    All California long.
Belief, an exhausted Chevrolet
With running boards and rings gone bad,
They call it Gypsy Rose Lee because
It's only got the bare essentials . . .
But takes them out answering orders
By traveling nights and sleeping days,
Helps detour them through one dull rental
After another for five years.

Later, an academic life.
They lose one child, have three more,
                                                progress,
Until the body's fractions add up
Against its certainties.
                    Sometimes
A radio left on all night
Because the weather's hot and still;
No one can sleep, but no one talks
Either.
        Or a dog barks at a car
Passing too slowly to be going
Anywhere but home, so late
That being late doesn't matter anymore.

Sometimes necessity becomes its own
Dwindling fact, like the stripper's need
For money,

         whose name they gave their car,
A joke to reconcile them to the things
They wanted then but couldn't have,
Like Kilroy, who only wanted to go home;

And beyond necessity, some hope
For other things put in the names
They gave to their children, to each other,
And the explanations handed their children
Because explaining things becomes
A way of naming them also.

Locked arms to pose a photograph
Surviving all these two survived,
No hint of what they saw ahead
Making them smile
                except
The camera's implicit place,
Circular and reflecting
Out of its own dark precision,
Dark like the theaters where people sat
Taking in short, censored newsreels
And narrow as the wised-up cold war
That followed,
             shadowing
The corny jokes on television,
Canned laughter over whiz-bombs, trick ties
With lights blinking across the *fifties*,
One whoopee-cushioned sigh of relief . . .

Like the relief reckoned by Gypsy Rose Lee
Writing her memoirs in 1955,
Addressing them to her son
And counting everything she owned,

Enumerating respectability,
The Rolls with matching luggage, the house
In New York on East Sixty-third
Complete with pool and elevator—
"Some little things removed,
Some big ones gathered up."

One innocence erodes another,
With neither one accurate in what
It pushes forward like a handbill
Or cart loaded with incidentals;
And no one cautions against the little things
Adding up in closets and storage rooms
To another set of incidentals,
Building toward one solemn rummage sale
Held, after the last big fire and funeral,
In everybody's yard,
                              but casual now
As a part-time worker taking orders
Or soldier on temporary duty,
Casual as someone sick
Who is left alone, dozing among
The pastel cards well-wishers have sent . . .

A several and sad innocence,
That spot an audience will watch
When a magic trick takes place,
Distraction made unique yet shared
And similar to the way you tighten
Inwardly to smile or seem natural
When someone takes your picture,
                              the day
Brought down to one approximation,
Leaving each one a little foolish,
Like a naked man whose navel's full of lint.

But in this photograph that's left
To me it's 1938.
                    Everything is
Ahead like something on a map
That someone reads in a car at night,
The road jostling a flashlight so
The map is hard to figure out,
This picture that they leave,
                              the one I find

Which now becomes a photograph I take
Of someone photographing me.
Cameras zoomed into each other,
Two lenses fix on interiors
That stop down to blank shutters cutting
Part to smaller part, like mirrors set
In a barbershop, facing
Their diminishing reflections.

Even diminishment provides
A kind of movement,
                    an always falling,
Like motion sickness,
                    but felt the way
An overloaded plane lifts off
Then doesn't climb but runs for miles
Barely above the trees until
Gathering speed
                the nose tilts up
And looking back you feel yourself
Dropping away
              through what you see.

The Distance into Place

Dolls in gallery along her walls,
She'd broken one so, bending down,
Opened a sewing box then knelt,
The needle's eye narrowing her gaze
To fractions in a room where clothes
And broken doll cluttered the floor.

Mid-thirties and already gray,
She focused on a wilderness
Of close particulars, a bird
Imagining a cage, her eyes
Turned like an animal's caught by
A car's headlights, reflecting blind
And lost inside the light they saw.
Later, the family away at church,
She used a butcher knife to carve
Initials in the dining room table.

On Sundays, we drove to Memphis
Where each visit I waited in the car,
Studying the windows I was told
Were hers, my talented aunt,
Playing the piano as soon as she
Could stand, homely, proud, and silent.
No photograph could get a smile.
The term I heard was that she was
Afflicted.
                    My parents spoke in fragments
As riding home I strained to catch
A phrase that held the syntax to her name.
Those trips, made thirty years ago,
We stepped out of our upright cars,
Mother and grandmother in hats and gloves,
My father smoking, fedora cocked

Ironically but eyes measuring
The distance out ahead as though
He walked into some fixed perspective.

Cold nights the house contracts
To the tightness of its carpenter's
Precise intent, leveled and squared
Again as if to match his mind.
A car's headlights scroll across the wall
As a figure deepens where curtains bell.
It bends and waves, ushering me
Beyond the place it disappears
Dark into dark and soft, a thing
Coagulate as guilt in memory,
As my aunt, childishly petulant yet old
And fluttering like an antique doll,
A miniature of iced velocities.

Broad day, I kneel to gather scrub
Grown up along the barbed-wire fence
That frames our farm. The fields
Are frozen hard, resistant as
The locust posts punctuating each fence.
The stream is skimmed with ice and makes
A fixed division of the land.
But night, when I wake to a figure
Idling across my wall, dissolving
Dark, the surface of that stream
Cuts to a slower, colder path.

One name becomes the secret to another,
Blue into gray, like rain, and gray
To deeper blue, till all the down-rush
We anticipate, the waking sleep of things,

Turns to a clarity like pain.
I see my aunt, alone and still,
Her room cluttered with the objects of
Intentions neither she nor her doctors knew
Because mutation made its own way
Through her life, carving its initials
As a code that waits inside a seed,
Its rope-like strands curling into thought,
That thought in turn a distance we contrive.

| Rooms without Walls

Late sunlight breaking into the room
And a boy's round face against the glass,
Breath clouding, eyes narrowed to the sun.
Outside, snow falls through the light;
The sky is granular and close,
All pattern of the wind's white slant,
That wind about the house, and branches'
Snow-muffled scrapes against the eaves.

Later, the power lines will fail,
And, twelve years old, I will stand outside
Counting the coal oil lamps that float
From room to room as though our house
Did not have walls inside but was
One space through which my family sent
Their liquid light without effort,
Like quiet conversation.

All this before the heart disease,
Cancers, and little suicides
Of cigarettes and whiskey turned
Events into a daguerreotype
Fading and slightly out of focus.
The snow, deeper than ever before,
Was in a frame I took outside
But never brought back in again.

Instead, with power lines knocked down
All over town, I stamped in the street,
My feet so cold they hurt, and gazed
Until I turned my family's warm house
Inside out, the snow's unfolding linen
And pillows deep as a child's gathering

Unconsciousness that sleeps through any sound
Made for the mind's stark furnishings.

Two blocks past where I stood, small shacks began,
Unpainted shotguns shouldered together
Into a row of narrow facings
I studied from the school bus window
Or counted as our car drove past—
Ten to a block, identical,
Each with its small front yard
Of bright red clay, as hard as pavement.

From that direction, over the stillness
The snow had brought, I heard the blows
And the high voice of a small girl
Who could not beg but only gasp
"Daddy, Daddy" between the cracking sounds
Made by whatever he'd picked up.
I stood more still than I had ever thought.
He beat her until there was silence.

And I think that action took forever.
More than the snow's cold multiplicity
Or all the lights that failed to work
In our small town, or hands that rested
In laps, in pockets, near telephones,
The hands of those who waited for
The power, thinking the novelty
Of such a deep snow, and that far south.

Later, unable to sleep, I stood
Listening as the cold house tightened and clicked
Down to the concentrated tense
Its builder meant, then from the hall the lights

Blinked on, blacked out, and I began to shake,
Not arms and legs but in the chest and gut.
The cold house clicked again, then stilled,
And when I closed my eyes light ran like iodine.

What I know now is that the frame
Made by the window where I stood
One afternoon was cold and arbitrary.
If anything, the snow's white sifting
Down my glass meant anonymity
Far past the best or worst we ever do,
Beyond all melting at our touch
Which like regret arrives past tense.

What I know is that our meanings work
Like games thought up by children in a street;
The space, number of players, goals
And objects moved are arbitrary,
And yet our games are serious,
As players go beyond themselves
Into a violence that wins,
And lets us say they were responsible.

The house I found that night was covered
By a snow that rounded everything;
No hedge or wall could separate its rooms
From a smaller space two blocks away,
The place of one small girl's high voice
Echoing the stillness that we are.

| Black Water

A fly on black water stands
Over himself on stilts, the poise
Of his slick reflection bobbing
Between water and eye, two mirrors
Facing an infinite digression.

How does the image he sees
Diverge into the things we name,
Eyes, thorax, spiracles? He strides
Water stilled under maples mixing light
Until one sees no separate thing.

All day trout glide silently beneath color
And reflected color where margins fail.
They swim with the heart's determined monotone,
Hungry for our imagist, who hovers
Light as the maple's paired wings and seeds.

The Gnostic at the Zoo

Man is the as yet undetermined animal.   —Nietzsche

Fat and bored, pedestrian
Behind their bars, they do not bear
The riddle that we bring
Like a twisted spine or guttural
Expressing pain before pain is felt.
Instead, they sleep and loaf beside
Their food, casual among the flies
And visitors circling them.

Cage after cage, we round corners
With soft-eyed generalities,
Puttering through catalogues of names,
But feel the harsh comparison
In the eyes of animals fed here
Reflecting like an old analogy.
Then beyond the elephants and giraffes
Exotic birds start chattering
As a young teacher leads her class
Of fourth graders past the cages,
Lecturing on Darwin and Lyell.

Eclectus Parrot, Paradise Whydah,
Purple Throated Euphonia . . .
Distinctions like the fretwork light
The parrots' cage extends across
The children's path mix in the shade
Of finger ferns hung overhead
Softening the heat and humidity
Of a summer afternoon into
The first savannah ever occupied.

They walk, then pause, then walk again,
Ignoring a polar bear's depressed
Indifference, the alligator's
Cold-blooded stare, then,
                          slowing,
Stop to study a half-grown chimpanzee
Hiding behind a tree, where,
In the mute extension of their seeing,
The green shade only moves one way.

I   A Retirement Catalogue

Brass telescopes with Halley on
The other end, chronometers
Inside their clear acrylic domes,
Tide charts, bird charts, thermometers,
A pendulum of solid chrome . . .
Items meant for a glass-topped desk
Or study window, the polished means
For measurement, a weather check
Without the weather, and time gleaned
By someone running out of time.

This catalogue was mailed to me
"Or Current Resident," in line
For leaving the line, my chance to see
How the list goes on into millions
And we barely stammer, distracted
By our small equipage, gadgets drawn
Ahead as if we had contracted
To make the count,
                              as setting out
Past where the roving jays will rout
And the windchimes clank without relief
The last page turns, the birds cry thief.

The Player Piano

Learning from a player piano,
I let my fingers rest on the keys
Until they drop from beneath into sound;
Inside, the mechanical works, set, greased,
And churning ahead of thought, possess
The future tense their builder meant
For the wires he chose, whose vertical stress
Tuned his wood, felt, and cogwheeled instrument.

A continuum of moving parts,
Music made without the variance
Of a slow hand or a false start,
How better to work one's will against chance,
Avoid the twelve-year-old who wrecks the scales,
Silence the adult whistling the *Vogelquartett*?
A century later, my fingers trail
Thought made mechanical, not grand but upright.

Wallace Stevens Remembers Halloween

for Bill Clarkson

The thing I loved was Halloween.
The children dressed in more colors
Than I could count, their multiples
Pressed in regiment, wedged and wiggling,
Masked giggles in the door's dark frame.
We'd have them in for cider, and,
Wearing my tuxedo, I'd bring the cups,
All stiff formality, but watching them
Lifting their masks to drink, catching their eyes.

Then off they'd go, their voices all
One high cacophony caroling
Into echoes, clamorous groups
With rumpled bags, each thrilled with his own
Anonymity on a night once meant
To celebrate the dead.
                              There are no dead,
Only the missing, and windows filled
With hollowed fruit and fire inside
Lighting our interrupted sleep
Much as comedians light laughter
From an audience's partial fears.

But those children made me glad.
I never thought behind the plastic grins
There were smiles waiting expectantly
For a hundred different futures,
For Halloweens no one could calendar.
I never took their peacock dress
And blackbird frequency as randomness,
As anything other than good fun
By miniature Taft Republicans.
They were my winter warblers, siskins
And kinglets, come to the comic feeder.

| Husband

Grief is this quiet room we shared,
Your heavy sleep my comfort even when
I lay awake because of you
And waited for the clock to close
My questioning that as a night light
Had the outline of our room but not its feel.
I waited till the birds outside
Began their widening paths for food
Then rose to make your breakfast,
A commonplace ignored yet needed.

Now the house will be too quiet,
Its rooms more spacious than before,
Evading my grasp like the shafts
Of light that skew this waking here alone.
I miss nothing you could give me
But your taking what I gave.

| Insomnia

Count the number of times boards crack
In the cooling house, or furniture plays
Like a thin percussionist tapping his way,
Working the bones over and back,
A blindman's stick or erratic clock,
The door that clicks in its frame as a key
Which someone works in your lock
Without forcing it, works patiently.

Two Kinds of Cause

for Barbara

Heaviest snow in years,
I drove at walking speed, my lights
Given back to me in thousands
Of particles, at once crystalline
And white and falling in a density
That blocked all but the wipers lazing
Across the glass
                    till home
I drifted right, bumped the curb and stopped;
Then picked a path along our drive ·
Noting the way each window's light
Worked differently across the snow,
Rectangular blues, purples, and yellows,
The landscape of a children's book
With pastel generalities
Rounding a world as soft as it was cold.

Later, walking outside again,
The snow had turned to freezing rain
Ticking into its own slick crust;
Then later still, another snow,
Granular down through the window's light,
Like white cells through an artery,
Leukemic in their mass and gathering.
I watched the trees and hedges bulge
Into a swollen weight that cracked
From branch to trunk to ground
Till something snapped, like burning grease
Or static. Ten feet away three wires
Snaked backwards, igniting where they touched.

Stepping away, I remembered what
I saw one night while walking home
With my father. An ambulance

Skidded into a pole and brought
High-tension lines down on its top.
Inside, the black driver was unhurt
But completely still, touching nothing;
The white man in back was dead but near
The lines and partly out a window.
The current made his body jump.
A man behind us laughed at this.
Another teased the driver, who sat
Expressionless, eyes straight ahead.

My father's hands were steering me
By the shoulders; we threaded through
The crowd, my head angled toward the wreck
Until we turned the corner to our street.
Once home, he used the telephone
Then carried me up to bed
Only to take a chair and talk
Long after I should have been asleep.
When I spoke, my voice was dry and thin;
His talking worked its way around
That change, floating a lower sound
Insistent and continuous,
Until beyond my questioning I slept.

What happened years ago came back
To me like something handed down.
From the snow-stilled street I turned and saw
Our house, first dark then one room with a light,
Then flashlights splashing down the hall,
Our children giddy in the dark.
Their lights bobbed then stilled beside the door,
Floating like the voice that once explained
Downed wires, wrecks, the cruelty of jokes,

The way things work when they don't work,
That voice building a screen that sieved
One sort of light and let me sleep.

The snow continued. I worked my way
Back to the house. The heat was out.
I built a fire and gathered blankets,
Thinking, first named by one then many,
We live out of two kinds of cause—
The snow collecting water for spring,
All colors held yet blank as bone,
The spectrum drawn back into white.

| Sisters

For you see they were to play in the Green Meadows all day long
until Old Mother West Wind should come back at night.

They are walking home in tight bunches,
Passing the football field where their brothers
Duck into helmets, like young goats who lunge
Head on. A whistle arcs and no one bothers
To check the time.
                        Then they are dressed
For a party that marks the end
Of a school year *everybody* passed . . .
Bright crinolined dresses casually flattened
Like wafers as they brush through doors
Opening to the stale gymnasium
Where their fathers chaperon a floor
That vibrates like a room-sized drum.

Escaping outside, they are children
Waiting for something they have never seen,
The moon flooding clouds that separate
Into brief, staggered patterns,
Prepotent figures in an old dance
Or young boys touching consequence,
The disparities of loss and birth,
Mother West Wind, Mother Earth.

| Saying It Back

One afternoon you step outside
To get the mail and see your son
Walking home, looking over his shoulder,
Calling to a friend who walks the other way.
And you double back into that time
When Mr. Ryland took you hunting,
Age twelve, because once years ago
Your grandfather had done the same for him;
And he cautioned you to look back every
Fifty steps, "to learn the woods past tense,"
He said. And so you walked ahead,
Gun barrel down and turning to look.
Later, game pouches stuffed with quail,
He let you lead the way across the field
Into the woods, and then into
All the backward glances you had made,
The trees dividing and birds scolding.

What is the lore to looking back like that?
Your son has barely moved from where
You saw him stepping off the bus.
First sight of him, his turning to call,
And you were twenty years away, at home
In Tennessee with Porter Ryland's father
Telling you how your grandfather
Could drop four quail with just three shots;
Telling you, the best way he knew how,
What to do when the covey flushed
Behind you; telling you who you were,
Till you had said your way back through the woods.

The Times Between

| The Kite

Away from playground games and fights,
He sings to himself, dancing in the grass,
Steps trailing, a single figure
Intent on the private craft of kites.

It flies because he will not let it go,
Because he wraps the twine around his hand
So tight that blood collects, darkening
Under the wind's insistent tug.

From liquid wrist the string dissolves into its length,
Its curve rising from the ground,
An anchored flight of immobility
And fragile parts strung taut to give them strength.

Vivid for the sky's emptiness,
A bright red patch against the haze and blue,
It soars along a shortened line, but falls
When given run before the wind;

Or like a solitary song's release,
The kite unreels along a spool of thread,
An outward surge over the wind
Flying by the force of being held.

The single master of a vacant lot,
By pulling down it rises up,
This craft of putting fragile things aloft,
Of letting go and holding on at once.

| Letter

Today the water whitens over rocks,
Breaking before our eyes into a sound
As constant as the rhythmed strokes
That neighbors make with saws, trimming the limbs brought down
By winter ice;
               the branches crack
As, thrown into the stream, they spin around
Then dart above rocks that, half submerged,
Jut moss-green from the mumbled blue, the current's urge.

Three days ago, two miles below the dam,
A boy slipped down in wading clothes,
Trout fishing with his father on the bank;
He surfaced, waved, then slipped again,
Tugging a canvas jacket free to swim.
His father ran along the edge
Then side-stepped to the middle with a limb.
The boy passed by head down.

Grappling lines dragged from either side,
They found him on the second day
Where, slowing, the river widens in a bend:
I stood among the trees and watched,
Immobile in the cooling shade;
He surfaced slowly, face up beneath a bridge
And eyes gazing beyond our grasp
As though he saw at once two sides of blue
And settled for the ground from which he slipped.

2

Cut limbs falling, the crack they make,
Each dropping from its trunk as though for once
The last branch winter made us trim
Was gone for good, more lightly lost for the violence
Of jagged saws, or spring turned whimsical.
The branches lopped, mid-air, mid-stream,
Are casual over the current's drag for them
Till underneath they tumble, breaking stem from stem.

Our stretch of it between the dam and bridge
Runs fast, the water like a path worn new,
Picking its way, wading the land,
As downward deep as upward blue,
At times almost reflecting where a bend,
Slowing, will make the surface calm.
Kept trim, the trees along each bank drink deep
As though one force, and always green, retained their seed.

A Family Portrait for Our Daughter

All night the nurses let me listen,
Your heart like hobnail boots down corridors.
The pain is rhythmical, and we talk between
Your urgencies, watching the clock
For more of you, pressed and pressing.
Positions much like tools with no handles,
Your mother shifts from chair to bed to chair,
Breathing with forced-march regularity.
Later, diminuendo on a side porch
Where instruments are fading out of tune,
The funny way the mind deflects from pain.
Then there you are, a late result
Of leisurely lust and evolution,
Your mother smiling over you
Out of the womb and endlessly crying;
Though innocent, already apprehensive.

Genetically, I'd mix you like Matisse
In a garden's green concert of senses,
Fluidity of feeling marveling where
The eye's despotic glance focuses then blurs.
Nearsighted, you cause us to draw close;
We wonder what you see of us,
A Dutch guild portrait with possessive eyes
Blinking each time the flash goes off?
Such pictures lie in spite of us.
Outside all photographs, this fact,
You cry full of a shower's present tense.

| The Namesake

A sister on the way, I was farmed
Out to my grandmother in Tennessee—
Picked Presbyterian her entire life
And reading Tennyson when I arrived
To spend all summer on her "home farm."
Once she taught Elocution to children
Who could not spell and whose "rise in life
Always stalled at local heights." They were determined.
And so was she, even reading "Tennusin"
With clipped enunciation.
                      But the world
I heard was never clipped; it ran beyond
The tree lines whose shadows framed the farm
Into a lush mid-air where all
Was waiting and nothing arrived.
Even the clock seemed stalled that summer,
As though we'd never get past 1954.

This year we skip the interstate,
Making our way rectilinearly
Back to the farm whose predestined crops
Grow like conservative bankers.
Another sister's on the way.
Her great-grandmother rises and stalls,
Greeting us through a screen; someone clips
The hedge beneath her window.
Beginning now, again life starts,
Swelling before a name, the seed so placed
That casually one bird alights,
Grasping the branch so many miss;
Much as an intervale crowds green each spring,
The snow's white riot flowered on the bough.
The water, having swollen into flood,
Resumes arterial calm, reflecting.

| The Effervescent Mrs. G.

Retainer of the bridge club win and loss.
Perhaps the numbing fall is always painless
Like a good block or uppercut
That knocked you out.

Regarding the scar of a Christmas sunset,
She said there was no fear of time
But there was always curiosity
For the hours spent over coffee or sherry.

When the obituary became
A catalogue of world events,
She would address a grandson with the name
Of his dead uncle, using a timeless logic.

She walked with the poise of a polite drunk,
The captain of a reeling deck;
Swaying in the hall mirror, she once remarked
That every house should have a picture window.

Lately, surveying the perimeters
Of an upstairs bedroom,
She addressed a ten-watt bed lamp
And wept for Jesus like a toy drum.

Her timeless dress and arrested smile
Have become frozen in the blue light
Of a diamond, a mirror,
A window's face framing the bland moon.

Bright curtains caught in an opened sash,
A curious love, curiosity kept her long
Living on coffee and sherry. But a cold
Scratched, filling one lung, then another.

I Domestic of the Outer Banks

For days the house is dark and slightly cold;
The wind is locked in curtains, in cupboards,
Is damply waiting on the cellar stairs
While fever burns beneath a single sheet.

She skims the room with shallow lungs for breath;
Her eyelids close by white and blue degrees
To patterns thrown upon a screen like paint,
Like aqua over sand in rhythmed sleep.

Here is the final illness of her age,
The pulse and watch unwinding into air
That waits between the walls and floors for fire,
For heat to draw the flesh to bony form.

Sick for an animate face
And single name to call this house,
Taut in the linen of a worn estate
With failing mind to grace the end, she waits

Condemned to province and imagined health:
Diluting measures of the medicine,
The lips drawn tight to smile,
She listens for familiar names and dates,

For sea gulls calling past the window sill
To hover and to plunge.
                              They plunge again
And she is thirty; the black-tipped birds
Are things that slice from air into the sea,

Are paring knives set to their memory.
The wings divide upon her severed air
Like hydras in a sensual wave
That will not unfold or give release.

The Vegetable Garden

Needled by death for change, for simple change,
We turn the soil,
                          another season's crop
Growing from seed, from rain and last year's rot
Into a fruit we never arrange:

The lettuce outgrows our appetite,
While fences smother with towering beans
And tomatoes swell from the dark of their roots;
All tactile reaching for decay turns green

And hangs in the spray of a garden hose.
Dripping with light, the leaves must bow,
Darkening under shadows we cast
Walking among each picked, each weeded row.

Seasons are canned into lines along shelves,
Are named and dated while vinegar boils,
Filling the house with an acrid smell,
And vines are turned beneath themselves:

Our garden is a form that answers cost,
And, growing out of hand with constant care,
Distinctions bloom, ripen, rot, and bear
Into the gathering grasp of something lost.

The Breaking Child

In my house the walls are not true;
Floors fit an oblique resolution
No carpenter's square can reconcile.
At night the wind whistles a crazy air,
And someone plays the sticks across the roof.
Ragtime gusting, the ridgepole dials
Under an incomplete geometry;
Shingle to shingle, the rhythm hoofs
A dance that is measured by miles.

My parents' furniture bulks where movers
Have left it. Unable to sleep, I trace
My hand on wood, deep-veined with burnishing.
Outside, the sky blows cold and clear;
Stars slue about the oblique foundation,
And the wind lobs limbs, waving,
Like upraised hands waving above a drop
Too deep to feel, yet welcoming connection.
Somewhere below a voice begins to sing:

And the house contains, all musicale,
The celestial spheres rolling from room
To room, unseasoned floor,
Defiant carpenter.
                    Whose hand-me-down is this?
Blue entering black, the sky is veined with limbs.
You, my parents, sing where wind has closed the door;
You grieve the tree line's seeded cut,
Years of fencing, the yard so hemmed
You stand apart looking beyond, living before.

I   An Intermittent Light

Evening paper under one arm,
I whistle my way briskly home.
The sun enlarges red till twice
Its size, the sky a dark relief
Of clouds knotting, then stretching from sight.
White pines still catch the sun's half disk
And burn with a green clairvoyance,
More fiercely for the shade they give.

Tonight the sky is translucent,
And houses wedge beneath as if
Diminished light intensified
Their interiors to certain space.

Rounding the corner to our street,
I wonder at our house, its small contrast.
Inside, you're sitting underneath a lamp;
The light is circular, and I am late
To a room that already arranges
Where we will sit and what we will say.

Think of the shadows underneath each tree
Dissolving, how the ambling mind
Must look for ways to cut beyond
Where, finding it circles, it fades;
Much as outside the window where we sleep
There are distances we never talk about,
Something in the way trees take the light
But, waking, we surface to their shade.

| Forest Fire

Set loose on the hills to tramp all night,
To crawl beneath the season's leaves
Or tower into trees with searing light
And breathe into a bright framework of limbs,

The fire proceeds before the wind,
A liquid light of tongue curled upon tongue
And waves of heat that hypnotize the eye,
That beckon one to walk within.

The blaze exhales and we retreat foot after foot
Like soldiers from an ancient war
With meaningless shields tempered to reason,
Reflecting the night's black wick and flame:

The leaves of every branch struck like a match,
The toppled oak consuming from the ground;
All night the hills are loud with falling trees,
Are bright with foliage eating from its branch.

The Widow's Halloween

The pumpkin's hollow head returns her gaze;
His yellow eyes are dancing in the flame,
And she, she has him on her windowsill
Within a draft that flickers on his brain.

His jagged smile and diamond eyes
Are mirrored in the darkened panes,
Set to be seen, not see, to blaze before the wind
Or wither on the wick and snap out cold.

Grinning backwards into the room,
On either side and looking in,
His gaze, she feels, was sharply cut
To burn beneath her dresses' hems

Or follow her when reaching for the broom.
She wears the latest fashions as her age
But feels the flicker of his gaze
And will not pass near him.

The Times Between

for Florence, Minnie, and Mary

The severe dancer poised before her mirror
Waiting for the music to begin;
Or academic nude, arms parabolic
Above the students of one pose:
For you that all was years ago,
Ward-Belmont, what little Nashville offered;
Half-gentlemen from Vanderbilt,
Starched collars bent to every healthy bustle.

Now it's the times between you must control.
Late afternoon when vacancy
Invades the room, even the sun porch
Lightens half-heartedly. It's like a lull
In conversation that's never taken up
But leaves each feeling vaguely responsible,
The retarded gust of a ceiling fan,
Too slow to cool, but always turning.

You, who taught us guilt and humor,
Your stories bringing laughter till we wept,
Would take us swimming, though afraid to swim;
Head heavier than feet, you said,
Don't go too far; and thus we always did.
Tonight, you swim beyond our call, and we
Must stand waiting. Regard us now,
Waving you towards the amplifying shore.

Caligula in Blue

What I have to tell you is the rain.
And that I am poor without you.
Here, the weather's all we reason by:
The sky blues overhead then clouds collect,
Our summer storms repeating themselves
Redundantly against the ground.
We look for rainbows out of here
In snapshots where the register is wrong;
I touch your picture by my bed
Then recollect myself and wait, listening.
The rain outside has drummed retreat.

Rain and the redundant ground,
Erosion is the only way we leave.
I hear hot water through the pipes
When I bathe, in my tropical ease;
The harbor's mouth is porcelain,
The drain's whirlpool, infinity.
Diminished apertures, I see myself,
A cavern finding water through a fault.

My roommate's like retarded light,
The landscape on a sill where dreams assert
An endless now. We sit in bed and watch
The Late Late Show, finding
The viewer's mind must frame and pan
Until the weather lets him sleep:
The rain spatters my notebook near a sash;
The manic wind is up, tearing leaves all night,
And I dream those leaves bleed and talk of you.

Awake at 6 A.M., the sky grays;
Blank aperture, then blank response,
Which makes me think the mind refracts itself

Discursively, in a round country
Where kind finds kind, and locks its gaze:
You've written me our daughter has my eyes,
My roommate has them too; he lounges
In a parrot shirt and reads my chart
Critically. Asked his name, he colors
Like a circus tent, then stammers
He has forgotten, but will remember.
When he can sleep, he dreams a rainbow;
Like mine, his spectrum is a glance turned blue.

My dear, the allegory in
My parrot talk has died here
Where doctors dart like sparrows, speaking
Prismatically, their conversations
Ranging over the months I can't recall
While, eraser clean, I kept my pencil sharp.
Why must the cogito and cockatoo
Always be caged together?
If mortality's the odd game love repays,
Why does the parrot shirt laugh blue when I weep fire?

| The Family Act

The big top billowing
over lines and poles,
its brightly colored
sections clash
as husband and wife
climb their ladder
and, introduced,
dive calmly into space.

Swinging above
the sawdust ground,
one meets the other,
catching her fall with
hand on wrist then,
turning around,
releases her
to twirl away.

The curve of the caught
fall is their serious play;
over a darkened ring,
the nets let down,
they live by taking
leave of those
who move them most
to stay.

The Nineteenth Hole

for Matt, left in Saigon

Now all the balls your daddy hit
Have been shagged. The nineteenth hole is
Full,
      and honor's safe on
The next golf cart teetering
Through the greening rough.
The bunker yawns unforgivably
As, putters out, a foursome ambles
Between dink shots on close-cut grass.

It is an old story that begins
With a boy whose father's mad and
Who stands outside a window listening to
The music inside. And there are grace notes
To this scene; a thrush hidden in a branch
Sings relentlessly, until the boy's gaze
Repeats itself in the darkened glass.

Years later, limbs circle in the wind
As mosquitoes bite like ideas in the dark
Of a porch arranged by rocking chairs.
Two figures talk beyond a lighted door,
Tilting over the rigid past
In chairs that arc outside of light,
Movement sweeping across wide fields
And dialogue that wills the years revoked.
Here, history is a common fault
Revised out of uncommon talk.
Your parents live along a gap that,
Waiting there, they cannot see yet argue for.

Watered by another generation,
The fairway's sown promise greens,
Though clipped too close to repeat itself.

Overhead, a low cloud's close approach,
Racing, is followed by cloud after cloud,
All racing, but to where?
And the general rain dispersing itself,
But toward what end?
One cell divides. Another dies.
The rhythm holds relentlessly.
Is it the ritual or narrative
Of our lives we understand?

| Towards a Relative Ending

Uninterrupted days occasion us,
Affording light, withdrawing light,
Almost as if someone too far away,
Had thought but then forgotten why he thought
Or, intuitive, had acted without cause
And, looking again, wondered what it was he meant.

Self-thinking and forgetful at one time,
We live in rooms we know too well
Until that ocular day,
Vivid for the sky's emptiness:
The desk no more a desk,
Bookshelves only a sequence after myth,
Each object odd, beyond the schemes
Of numbered space and alphabet;

Or else a room kept closed too long,
A safe appointed place
Imagined as the portal to some end
With light obscured by canopies of dust,
An iridescent dust in winter light
That suddenly draws dark along the floor,
Clouds passing miles overhead.

| Our Tree of Opposites

I watch you where the wren will wake
Restless and alert, your laughter rising
Above the ash and evergreen,
The wren's insistent music rising
And branches sculling, oars against wind,
A changing current, leaves lifting with
A gust that never circles back.

The weather turns. The season turns,
March into April, limbs fingering leaves
That silhouette reticulate shade
Across the raveled undergrowth;
A reed thrumming in the wind
And the bird, head tilted, watching you,
Your voice cutting inside a shadow's edge.

Most days our tree of opposites
Thickens with a reasoned fruit,
Two names balancing solecisms
Under the limb-divided sky.
The wren sings. You stand apart.
I follow a path that runs interior;
The animal I find stands reflexively.

At night, we wait to brave a sleep
That interlocks all the day divides.
Outside, the ash and evergreen are tilting:
In the woods an animal dies,
And seeds take root in the decay until
A tree towers. When light unfolds that tree
The wren will wake and each of us will sing.

| ACKNOWLEDGMENTS

Some of the poems in this volume were previously published, some in slightly different form, in the following, to whose editors grateful acknowledgment is made: "Husband," *Agenda*; "Learning the Bicycle" and "A Note of Thanks," *American Scholar*; "Late Fall, Late Light," published as "Fall," *Boulevard*; "Haying," *Bread Loaf Anthology*; "The Vegetable Garden," *Canto* and *The Oxford Book of Garden Verse*; "A Family Portrait for Our Daughter," *Chariton Review*; "The Old Cadets," *Chattahoochee Review*; "March," *Connecticut Review* and *The Best American Poetry, 1998*; "Cousins, Brothers, Sisters" and "Reading before We Read, Horoscope and Weather," *New Criterion*; "The Downtown Bus," *Five Points*; "Elderly Lady Crossing on Green," *The Formalist*; "The Kite" and "Our Tree of Opposites," *Georgia Review*; "Playing by Ear," "The Pyromaniac," and "The Wild Horses," *Kenyon Review*; "The Widow's Halloween," *Michigan Quarterly Review*; "Grown Men at Touch," *New England Review*; "A Baseball Team of Unknown Navy Pilots, Pacific Theater, 1944," "The Distance into Place," "Oh General, Oh Spy, Oh Bureaucrat!," "Thaumatrope," and "The Widow's Halloween," *New Republic*; "The Depression, the War, and Gypsy Rose Lee," *New Virginia Review*; "Black Water," *New Yorker*; "The Books," *The Oxford American*; "The Poem," *Oxford Poetry*; "The Gnostic at the Zoo," "A Retirement Catalogue," "Saying It Back," "Sisters," "Two Kinds of Cause," and "Wallace Stevens Remembers Halloween," *Parnassus*; "Insomnia," *Poetry Now*; "Letter," "Domestic of the Outer Banks," and "The Vegetable Garden," *PN Review*; "The Covined Bird" and "The Name," *Reaper*; "Elderly Lady Crossing on Green," "The Ferris Wheel," "Insomnia," "A Note of Thanks," "Reading before We Read, Horoscope and Weather," and "A Winter's Tale," *Rebel Angels*; "Towards a Relative Ending," *Salmagundi*; "Blood," "Eyeing the World," "The Player Piano," "The Times Between," "The Window Washer," and "A Winter's Tale," *Sewanee Review*; "Sequence," "Since the Noon Mail Stopped," and "The Taking Down," *Sewanee Theological Review*; "Baseball," "Caligula in Blue," "Dr. Williams' Garden," "Domestic of the Outer Banks," "Extravagant Love," "Falling through the Ice," "Haying," "Late Days," "Letter," "This," "Water," "The Water Slide along the Beach," and "Yes," *Southern Review*; "Rooms without Walls," *Tendril*; "Coach" appeared in the anthology, *Unleashed* (Crown, 1995); "A Box of Leaves," *Verse*; "The Effervescent Mrs. G." and "Forest Fire," *Virginia Quarterly Review*; "The Lake House" and "Seasons," *Yale Review*.

Poetry Titles in the Series

Library of Congress Cataloging-in-Publication Data

Prunty, Wyatt.
   Unarmed and dangerous : new and selected poems /
   Wyatt Prunty.
       p.   cm. — (Johns Hopkins, poetry and fiction)
   ISBN 0-8018-6290-6 (alk. paper)
   I. Title.   II. Series.
PS3566.R84U53   1999
811'54—dc21   99-27613

Made in the USA
San Bernardino, CA
25 May 2017